LOUISIANA LONGSHOT

JANA DELEON

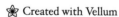

CHAPTER ONE

I STEPPED OFF THE LEARJET AT THE PRIVATE AIRFIELD JUST before dawn. I'd been on the plane exactly seventeen hours, twenty-six minutes and fourteen seconds, wearing the same eight-hundred-dollar dress I'd worn when I killed a man twenty-five hours earlier. One of my shoes hadn't made it out of the desert, and I clutched what remained of the other shoe in my right hand and my nine millimeter in the left. Apparently, eight-hundred-dollar dresses didn't come with pockets or holsters, and I didn't have the kind of cleavage that made a viable hiding place.

A black Cadillac DTS with limo-tinted windows waited at the end of the runway, so I took a deep breath and headed for the car, steeling myself for the ass-chewing I knew was coming. But when I opened the door and slid into the passenger's seat, the angry, balding man I'd expected to see was nowhere in sight. Instead, a slightly overweight, fiftyish, African-American woman frowned at me, shaking her head.

"Girl, you are in one heap of trouble," said the driver, Hadley Reynolds, CIA executive assistant extraordinaire.

"Did he have a heart attack when he heard?" I asked,

1

wondering why the director had sent Hadley instead of coming himself. "I figured he'd be here to run me over with the car."

"He had a moment there during that phone call when I wondered. His face turned so red, I thought he was going to pop, but then he rushed out yelling at me to pick you up and take you to meet him as soon as you arrived."

I sighed, my fleeting thoughts of a real meal and decent clothes slipping from my mind. Not only had the plane been stocked with healthy food, it hadn't contained an ounce of alcohol. "I guess picking up a burger and six-pack on the way is out of the question?"

"It's six a.m."

"Not in the Middle East," I pointed out.

"This is Washington, D.C., not some giant sandbox. Besides, you're meeting at a café. You can have all the fat and carbs you want." Hadley looked down at her own plump figure then over at me and frowned. "You know, I rarely ask for anything although I do a lot of favors—and God knows, I'm never going to fit in one of those size-four dresses they put you in—but why can't you be kind to the shoes?"

I looked down at what was remaining of the Prada shoes and felt a bit guilty. When I'd opened the box containing the shoes at CIA headquarters, I thought Hadley was going to pass out. She'd stared at them as if they were magical. My reaction hadn't been exactly the same. "I'm sorry."

Hadley raised one eyebrow.

"I swear. I'm sorry. That entire situation got a little out of hand. I didn't plan on ruining the shoes."

Hadley sighed and patted my leg, like she'd done since I was a little girl. "Honey, I know you didn't, but you keep having these *situations*. I'm afraid that one day I'm going to be picking you up in a box."

"It's my job."

"The risks you take are not your job and you know it." She

paused for a couple of seconds. "You don't have anything to prove...not to him or anyone else."

I just nodded and looked out the window, not wanting to get into a discussion about my late father, the "him" in her statement. Even though he died when I was fifteen, I could still see him frowning at me and shaking his head. Unfortunately, I couldn't blame him. Super CIA agent Dwight Redding had never made a mistake, never blown his cover, and never killed someone who wasn't on the hit list.

Dwight Redding had been perfect. The golden boy at the CIA.

Changing mental channels, I focused on the current situation. "Why a café?"

"The director didn't say."

I studied Hadley's expression, but she was telling the truth, which worried me even more. If Director Morrow wanted to meet with me somewhere other than CIA headquarters that could mean only one thing—he was letting me go.

I sucked in a deep breath and blew it out slowly, trying to prepare my defense argument. Best to hit him with it first, before he could pull the trigger—play to his sympathies. Yeah, that was it. If, of course, I could figure out exactly what his sympathies were before we got to the café. Eight years of working for him hadn't provided a single clue.

Hadley made a sudden turn and pulled up in front of a dingy storefront with the day's special painted right on the grimy window. "You sure he's not going to kill me?" I asked, giving the neighborhood a quick once-over. It looked like the kind of place where no one would blink over the sound of gunshots.

Hadley shook her head. "If the director doesn't kill you, the food in there probably will."

"Thanks for the vote of confidence." I climbed out of the car, leaving the broken shoe behind, and headed into the café.

I spotted Director Morrow and another agent, Ben Harrison, in a booth at the back of the single room. Otherwise, it was completely empty. Morrow frowned as soon as he saw me walk in. As I got closer, he noticed my bare feet and downed his entire glass of water. I glanced over at Harrison, trying to get a read on Morrow's state of mind, but he gave me an imperceptible shake of his head. Not good. Time for defense mode.

"I had to kill him," I said as Harrison rose and allowed me to slide into the booth across from Morrow. "I didn't have a choice."

Harrison made a choking sound, sat down next to me and had a fake coughing fit into his napkin.

"Your personnel file," Morrow said, "is full of those 'no choice' situations. Your hit count makes Attila the Hun look like a pacifist."

"But he was going to sell that girl to the sheikh. She was only twelve years old and -"

"I don't care if he had Siamese twins with puppies. You *always* maintain cover." He held up two fingers. "Two years worth of work blown in less than a minute. It's a new record, Redding."

"I can still salvage it. Just put me back in."

"How do you propose I do that? You were *supposed* to be the distributor's new eye-candy. All you had to do was deliver the money, collect the drugs, and leave. But no, you had to kill the brother of the boss...an arms dealer who shot his wife for walking in front of the television during American Idol. Do you really think he's going to give you a pass on killing his only sibling?"

"Not to mention," Harrison added, "that most hoochies don't go around killing people with their shoes. He's probably figured out you're not some ditzy gold digger."

I glared at Harrison, who only seemed to have diarrhea of

the mouth when it involved me. "There wasn't any place on my body I could hide a gun—not with that sleazy dress I had to wear. And that shoe had a spike on it. What the hell else is it good for?"

"Jesus, Redding." Harrison laughed. "Haven't you seen a movie, a magazine ad...another woman in public? Stilettos are common among people with estrogen."

"Which explains why *you* know what they are, and I don't. Why don't you play the girl on the next mission? You're obviously better suited."

"There is no next mission," Morrow said, cutting off the argument altogether.

I whipped around to face the director. "You're firing me? You can't do that."

"I could do that if I wanted to, but that's not the problem. We got news from Intel this morning. Your face has been distributed to every drug and arms dealer that does business with Ahmad's organization. He's offering one million to anyone who brings your body to him. Ten million if someone brings you in alive."

"Jesus," Harrison said, all antagonism gone.

I felt the blood start to drain from my face, and mentally tried to force it back up. "So? It's not the first time an agent has had a price on their head," I said, hoping my voice sounded stronger than I felt.

Morrow shook his head. "We've never had a case this bad. Seeing you dead has become the personal agenda of one of the biggest arms dealers of the decade. I have no choice but to make you disappear."

"No way am I going into witness protection. They'll stick me in some bank teller job in Idaho."

"I agree that witness protection is out, but not because I care what job you'd be asked to perform." Morrow leaned across the table, his expression a combination of serious, concerned, and just a hint of fear. It was the fear part that made my breath catch in my throat.

"There's a leak," Morrow said, his voice low. "I know it's coming from inside the CIA, but have no idea how high up it goes."

I gasped, my mind trying to grasp what he'd said. It wasn't possible. A traitor in the agency?

"No way!" Harrison jumped up from the booth and paced in front of it. "I don't believe it."

Morrow sighed. "I didn't want to believe it, either, but the reality is, someone put Ahmad's people onto Redding before she ever set foot on that boat. That whole scene with the girl was intentional—trying to force Redding to blow her cover so they could be certain. They knew she didn't have a gun, but apparently didn't factor in how dangerous she was in high heels."

"Shit," Harrison said and slumped back down in the booth.

Morrow looked at Harrison then back at me. "Both of you know that information about the mission could only have come from our office. According to Intel, Redding wasn't supposed to make it off that boat at all, much less alive. And that whole shoe incident upped the stakes astronomically."

"She can have plastic surgery," Harrison said. "It's done all the time, right?"

"No way!" I argued.

Morrow held up a hand to stop the exchange. "You've been watching too many Hollywood movies. Plastic surgery can't change her height or her bone structure, not enough, anyway. Ahmad's security equipment is top of the line. A single photo taken by one of his cameras, and they'd have the bone structure pinned right back to Redding. We still have another operative inside. We can't afford the risk."

"So, what am I supposed to do?" I asked, the gravity of the

situation finally sinking in. "You're telling me I'm not even safe at CIA headquarters? Where am I supposed to go?"

Morrow pushed a folder across the table. "I have an idea," he said somewhat hesitantly. "It wouldn't be official. Only you, me, and Harrison would know about it. That's why I'm speaking to the two of you here. I can't trust anyone else, and there's the possibility that my office is bugged."

Harrison glanced over at me and nodded. "Whatever you think, sir. I'll do whatever you need."

"All I need from you, Harrison, is to keep your mouth shut and remember this information in case something happens to me. For the obvious reasons, there will be no paper trail. Redding, on the other hand, is going to have to do a bit of maneuvering to pull this off."

"Pull what off?"

"My niece just inherited a house from her maternal great-aunt. She's scheduled to spend the summer at the place, going over the contents and getting it ready to sell. She's never been there before, and my understanding is the aunt wasn't the picture-hanging kind of gal, so there's very little risk of anyone catching on."

"Catching on to what, exactly?"

Morrow blew out a breath. "I want to send my niece to Europe for the summer, and I want you to go to Louisiana and pretend to be her. It's the perfect cover. No one will be looking for you there, and no one in the town has ever met my niece. They just know she'll be arriving sometime this summer to settle things."

"Louisiana...you mean swamps and alligators and hicks?"

"I mean a small town with lovely people and a slower pace. Just until we've removed Ahmad. The hit on you is personal. Without Ahmad in charge, the hit will likely go away."

My mind began to whirl again. "But that could be weeks... months. You can't expect me to live in the middle of a swamp for that long. What in the world would I do? They probably don't even have cable television. Is there electricity? Oh my God, isn't that where they filmed *Deliverance?*"

Morrow shot me a dirty look. "You've spent days crawling through the desert with only a rifle and a bottle of water. Don't tell me a couple of blue-haired old ladies and some mosquitoes are going to be the death of you. This is a vacation compared to your norm."

He pointed to the folder. "This is some background information I put together on my niece. Her aunt probably talked about her, so the townspeople will be looking for someone meeting that description."

"What about the Internet?" Harrison asked. "Most people are all over it."

Morrow shook his head. "She had a stalker situation when she was a teen that scared her senseless. She's been diligent about keeping herself off the Net. I've already checked and it's clean."

Morrow looked at me. "I need you to be ready to leave by tomorrow."

I reached for the folder, making note of the fact that Morrow was looking off at the wall behind me rather than looking me in the eye. Not good. A feeling of dread washed over me as I opened the folder and started to read.

Sandy-Sue Morrow. Good God, the name alone stopped me cold.

I kept reading and felt the blood drain from my face. Finally, I looked up. "I can't do this."

Harrison, sensing something was seriously screwed, looked from Morrow to me, waiting for the dam to break. "You're a professional," Harrison said. "You're a genius at undercover work—well, sorta."

"This," I said and shook the file, "is not undercover. *This* would require a reincarnation."

"Now, Redding," Morrow began.

"She's a librarian," I interrupted. "The last thing I read was an article on making a silencer out of a Q-tip, unless you count autopsy reports."

"You're going to inventory a house, not run a library" Morrow pointed out. "No one's likely to ask you for reading recommendations."

"She knits."

"So you'll learn, just in case. It wouldn't hurt you to have a hobby besides racking up bodies."

Harrison shook his head. "I don't know, sir. I've seen those knitting needles. Do you really think you should turn Redding loose on an unsuspecting population and give her a weapon? Remember that incident in Egypt with the No. 2 pencil?"

"Don't be ridiculous," I snapped. "That was a Pentel, not a No. 2."

Morrow cleared his throat. "I'm sure Redding will find a way to contain herself."

I tossed the folder back across the table. "She was a beauty queen!"

"Holy shit." Harrison dissolved into a fit of laughter. "No way is Redding pulling that one off. Look at her. Her hair's shorter than mine."

"My hair is convenient for my job," I said, running a hand over inch-long, blond locks that had been trapped under a hot wig the day before, "and besides, I thought short hair was fashionable."

"Short, yes," Harrison said, "but you're sporting the Britney Spears Nervous Breakdown style. *Not* a hit among men or the beauty pageant circuit."

I threw up my hands. "This...this *person* has single-handedly set the women's movement back ten years. Knitting? Librarian? Beauty queen? Please tell me I can kill her next."

Morrow rose from the booth and glared down at me. "That

will be enough. My niece is a lovely woman. And until further notice, you will become that lovely woman, or I will shoot you myself."

"You could try," I mumbled.

"What?"

I bit the inside of my lip and clenched my hands. "No problem."

"Good. Your afternoon is booked. You're getting acrylic nails, a pedicure, hair extensions, and learning how to apply makeup and wear high heels without killing someone." He gave me a broad smile then walked out the door.

Harrison gave me a sideways glance and inched away from me in the booth. His hand hovered over his weapon as he made a break for the door behind Morrow.

Fake hair? Fake nails? Someone touching my feet? Oh, God, they were going to paint my toenails pink, weren't they?

I groaned and placed my head on the table, covering it with my arms. This was going to be even harder than the time I killed that drug lord with a Tic Tac.

And not nearly as satisfying.

CHAPTER TWO

On a hot and humid Saturday evening, I stepped off the bus in Sinful, Louisiana, and was fairly certain I'd gone straight to hell. Forrest Gump had gotten it all wrong. Life wasn't a box of chocolates. It was a box of ex-lax, and I felt like I'd consumed the entire thing.

I stared down Main Street and grimaced. It was a cross between a Thomas Kinkade painting and a horror movie. A pretty, pink store with lacy-looking trim sat at the end of town. Pots of flowers rested along the sidewalk in front of the store. The sign in the window read, You Kill 'em—We'll Stuff 'em. A giant deer head with crossed eyes hung next to the entry.

The shop next to it was all brick, painted pale blue with navy edging. No potted plants there, but ivy with cute, little white flowers grew up the front of the building to a terrace on the second floor. The sign in that building's window had an arrow pointing to the pink store and read, Give 'em the Skin— Give Us the Meat. I hoped to God it was a butcher shop.

"Here's your luggage, ma'am." The voice of the bus driver sounded behind me and shook me out of my Alice in Wonderland moment. I looked back at the two bright pink suitcases with silver, tinsel tassels and choked back a wave of nausea. While I'd been tortured by the women at that salon, Harrison had been sent luggage shopping. This was his final parting shot.

I'd have rather it came from his nine millimeter.

I thanked the bus driver and handed him a big tip. If I never returned from here, I needed someone to remember where they'd seen me last. I extended the roller bar for the large case and placed the smaller one on top of it, trying not to notice my long, painted nails. I'd asked for black polish, but Morrow had called ahead and warned them. They'd offered me wine and little froufrou cakes and thought they'd get me to go along with "Delicate Mauve" or "Sunshine Tangerine," but I was onto them. We finally compromised on "Ravishing Red," a shade I picked because it was the exact color of freshly-spilled blood.

I pulled a piece of paper from the pocket of my ghastly purple suit and studied the directions. My "great-aunt's" house was probably a mile from here, which wouldn't have been a problem under normal circumstances. Under normal circumstances, I'd single-handedly overturned dictatorships in *less* than a mile. But in a polyester suit, in the dead heat of Louisiana, and wearing high heels, I'd be lucky to make it down Main Street without stabbing myself with that deer head's antlers just to end it all.

Sighing, I grabbed the handle of my luggage. I managed two steps before my ankle twisted and the heel broke right off the damned shoe. *Two hundred dollars for that piece of crap.* I didn't even want to think about the silencer I'd been looking at for less than that, or the black market grenades I could have added to my illegal collection.

I picked up the broken heel, pulled off both shoes and chucked them into a stream of dirty water that ran the length of the town behind the kill-'em-and-eat-'em shops. Yet another pair of fancy, overpriced shoes that Hadley would never get to wear.

"I'd hate to see you arrested for polluting the bayou your first day in town," a man's voice sounded behind me.

I whirled around, angry that someone had managed to get so close to me and I hadn't even been aware of his existence. The fact that he was driving a huge truck with obscenely large tires just reinforced my belief that after five minutes in Louisiana, I'd already lost my edge.

I gave the man a quick assessment—*mid-thirties, six foot two, about twelve percent body fat and has a blind spot forty-five degrees off center in his left eye.* A weakness I could capitalize on.

"Polluting?" I inquired. "I just increased the value of that mud stream."

He smiled—one of those patronizing, fake smiles that men used only on what they mistakenly assumed was the weaker sex. "That mud stream feeds half the people in this town."

"I'm on a diet."

"You must be Marge Boudreaux's niece."

It took me a moment to realize that the "Boo-drow" that came out of his mouth equaled the "Boudreaux" I'd read in the obituary, but I'd never have gotten that right. "Yes."

"Bet you're wondering how I knew."

"Well, the whole town is probably comprised of fifteen people and whatever they shot yesterday, and since none of them walk down Main Street with pink luggage—at least I hope not—I'm not exactly amazed that you realized I was a stranger."

He raised his eyebrows. "Marge described you as a lot nicer. Guess she meant compared to her. Well, since you're here...and barefoot, I'll be happy to give you a lift. That gravel is rough on the feet."

I looked down at the road, realizing for the first time that I wasn't standing on pavement. Instead, my feet were firmly planted on some strange mixture of dirt and shells. Thank God that pedicure hadn't made pansies out of my feet. "I'm fine, really."

He didn't look the least bit convinced, but apparently figured he'd done his southern duty. "Okay. Well, see you around." He pulled away, the ridiculously huge tires of his truck stirring up more dust than a desert storm.

For a shot of whiskey and a pair of combat boots, I'd have grabbed the tailgate of Bubba's truck and rode my luggage to the other side of town. But then that might have stood out. Likely, librarian ex-beauty queens didn't ride luggage.

Twenty minutes later, I strolled up the walkway of my new residence. It was a huge Victorian, and I sighed in relief that it was painted a sensible navy blue and contained no flowers in pots or in the front landscape that I'd likely kill. Now if only the inside was fern- and ivy-free, I was in business.

Fifteen more steps and I could get inside, out of public view, change into normal clothes and wait until midnight to burn the luggage in the backyard. I could already smell the smoke. But when I placed one foot on the porch, the front door opened and a little, white-haired, old lady stepped out.

Five foot two, a hundred and ten pounds with the purse, older than Christ, too many weak points to name.

"You must be Sandy-Sue." The woman stepped forward to clutch my hands. "I'm so happy to finally meet you. I was afraid your bus had been delayed."

"Nope. Right on time." *Like rushing toward death.*

"Wonderful. I'm Gertie Hebert, one of your aunt's oldest friends."

I nodded. The emphasis was on *old*.

Gertie reached into a huge handbag that looked like it was made from tapestry and dug out a Baggie. "Caroline had a chicken incident over at her place and didn't get to making the welcome basket, so I had to improvise." She held out the Baggie. "Prune?"

"Maybe later," I said. *Like when I'm ninety*.

"Well, then come on inside and meet Bones. Maybe we can dig you a pair of shoes out of that interesting luggage of yours. You know, women haven't been required to go barefoot in Sinful for at least forty years."

I stared. "Are they still required to be pregnant?"

Gertie waved a hand in dismissal. "Only if you were born on the first Tuesday of the crawfish festival, and then only if there was a full moon. But there's probably an exception with you being from out of town and all." She turned around and entered the house.

For the first time in my life, I felt a small tremor of fear trickle down my spine. I'd obviously crossed into enemy territory, and darned if I hadn't tossed my only weapons in that muddy water.

I stepped inside the house, relieved that there weren't a bunch of antiques or glass sitting around and surprised by the understated furniture and light tan walls. Not a tassel or bit of lace in sight. I just might be able to manage this.

"This is pleasant," I said.

"You sound surprised."

"Yes—No...Well, I figured, given that the rest of the town looks like a pastel painting..."

Gertie nodded. "You know Marge wasn't exactly a follower. She didn't like gardening or cleaning, so she wasn't about to have 'shit that needed watering or dusting' around her place." Gertie grinned. "Marge was a bit of a feminist. Ahead of her time, really, but then I'm not telling you anything new."

I felt my spirits rise a bit. Maybe, just maybe, this wouldn't turn out to be awful.

"I made coffee," Gertie went on as she waved for me to

follow her down a hallway off the front living area. "Marge was always worried about you, dear."

"Me?" I walked through a doorway behind Gertie and stopped short to look at the bright, sunny kitchen. The walls were painted off-white; the cabinets were oak and real hardwood, not the fake crap like I had in my apartment back in D.C. Miles of granite countertops covered the cabinets forming an L shape around the kitchen area.

"Yes, dear," Gertie poured a cup of coffee and set it on the countertop in front of me, then placed a wooden box of sugar and cream next to the coffee.

I ignored the sweetener, took a big sip of the coffee, and sighed with pleasure. Gertie made coffee that would strip paint off a bumper.

Gertie watched me for a moment, then poured herself a cup of coffee. "Marge was concerned that you wouldn't live up to your potential as a woman. She thought you had some old-fashioned ideas." Gertie looked at the unused sweetener, then back at me, and smiled. "Maybe she was wrong."

Uh-oh. I scrambled for an explanation. I hadn't even been in Louisiana thirty minutes and already someone was onto me. If I couldn't fool Mother Time, how was I supposed to fool anyone else? "My, uh, mother, had a different view of things than Aunt Marge."

Gertie nodded in understanding. "And you did what good daughters do and went along with her. Of course, dear, I understand that completely. My mother had ideas of her own, too. I was a constant trial to her."

"You? What in the world did you do?"

"I didn't get married and give her grandchildren. Why that was a mortal sin to Mother. A woman who couldn't find a man was to be pitied."

"You don't strike me as someone I should pity."

Gertie's eyes twinkled. "Smartest thing I ever did was not

have a man. I've had seventy-two years of doing what I please."
She patted my hand. "You and I are going to get along just
fine."

I felt a shift somewhere in the universe, and smiled at
Gertie. Maybe, just maybe, this wouldn't be so bad after all. I
was just about to ask for a second cup of coffee when a lump of
blankets in the corner of the kitchen shifted and rose from the
box they were in. I barely kept myself from reaching for the
weapon that wasn't there and instead pointed to the corner.

Gertie glanced at the box, then the clock. "Five p.m. on the
dot. Time for Bones to get some exercise." Gertie walked over
to the corner and pulled the blankets off the box. Finally, a
hound dog's head emerged. He stared at me for a moment, and
I wondered if he was a trained attack dog, but when he took
the first shaky step out of the box, I realized the dog was old.

"I guess I know why they call him Bones," I said, taking in
his thin, bony frame.

"Oh, that's not why," Gertie said. "He was a magnificent
piece of hound in his day, but Bones is getting up there." She
opened a door at the back of the kitchen and the dog strolled
outside. Gertie motioned to me and we stepped out
behind him.

Bones did the whole sniffing routine at the edge of the
bushes, then leaned against the side of the back porch to prop
himself up and hike a leg. The necessary business completed,
he then headed toward the dirty stream that ran across the
back of the lawn.

"Is that the same dirty water running through town?" I
asked.

"Yes, that's Sinful Bayou. Creates a bit of a problem with
mosquitoes and snakes, but alligators rarely come into the
lawns, so you probably won't have to worry about that."

Oh goody. I might not have to kill anything my entire visit.

Bones waded at the edge of the bayou and stood there as if

he were soaking his feet. His head was down, with his nose close to the surface, but he wasn't drinking. Thank goodness. Lord only knew what was in that water besides my shoes.

Gertie frowned. "There he goes again. That dog."

"What's he doing?" I asked, just as Bones began to dig. "Is he going to be all right? He looks like he's going to drop any minute." The dog wobbled like a drunk, throwing water and dirt around him at a faster pace than I would have thought him capable of.

Gertie waved a hand in dismissal. "He does it all the time. Tracks mud everywhere."

All of a sudden, he stopped and put his nose right up to the surface of the water, then completely submerged his head in the murky mess. A couple of seconds later, his head popped up with a large white object in his mouth. Looking extraordinarily pleased with himself, he trotted back to where we stood, dropped the object at our feet, and shook bayou water on us.

I put one hand up to shield my face and looked down as Bones dropped on his belly and began gnawing on one corner of the object. "Gertie? That's a bone."

Gertie lowered her hand and looked down at the hound. "Well, of course it is. We had to install cement footers around the entire cemetery because of that dog. How do you think he got his name?"

I narrowed my eyes at the object between Bones' paws, making certain my initial thought was correct. "You sure those footers went around the entire cemetery?"

"Yes. Why do you ask?"

"Because that bone is human."

CHAPTER THREE

GERTIE STARED AT THE BONE, THEN BACK UP AT ME, AND FOR a moment, I was afraid the prunes were going to repeat on her. The color drained from her face and she whispered, "What do we do?"

"Did you kill him?"

Gertie's eyes widened and she sucked in a breath. "Lord no! I...I don't...I can't..."

"Then we call the police. You have police here in Mayberry, right?"

"Of course. We have the sheriff and a deputy."

"Then let's head inside and dial them up."

"What about the...you know? We can't just let Bones keep gnawing on it. I mean, that's someone's family."

I took a look at the hound, who was stretched out on the lawn, gnawing the bone in slow motion and about to nod off to sleep. "I don't think he's going to do much damage. He probably doesn't even have any teeth left."

Gertie didn't look convinced, but she trailed after me as I headed back inside the house. I located the phone at one end of the kitchen counter and passed it over to Gertie, then proceeded to fix myself another cup of coffee. It was going to be a long evening.

Gertie took the phone, then bit her lower lip. "Maybe I should call Ida Belle."

I paused before taking a sip of coffee and looked over the cup at Gertie. "Your sheriff's name is Ida Belle?"

"Of course not. Robert E. Lee has been the sheriff here forever."

I blinked. Surely she meant figuratively. "So why would you call this Ida Belle before you called the sheriff?"

"Ida Belle is the president of the Sinful Ladies Society."

I waited a couple of seconds for more information, but apparently Gertie thought that one sentence had explained it all. "So, this Ida Belle will call the sheriff—measure the bone for a slipcover...or what?"

"Ida Belle will do whatever is necessary. The Sinful Ladies Society has been running Sinful since the sixties. I know the mayor likes to think he and the city council have a say, but everyone's just humoring them."

"Of course," I said, even though I had absolutely no idea what was going on in this town. "Maybe call the sheriff first, then Ida Belle. Keep up the illusion for the men?"

Gertie nodded. "That's a sound plan. Keeping men in line requires a delicate balance."

She started pressing numbers on the phone, then paused. "I'm wondering...why did you ask me if I'd killed that person?"

"Because I needed to know whether to call the police or help you hide the body."

Gertie's face cleared in understanding and she smiled. "Of course."

I didn't know whether to be relieved or afraid.

Apparently, Saturday afternoons were a hotbed of criminal activity for Sinful, so we had to wait almost an hour before the sheriff showed up. He looked nothing like the pictures of Robert E. Lee from my history books, but he did ride up on a horse. Ida Belle, on the other hand, had shown up within minutes, her white hair wrapped around giant rollers and covered with a bright green scarf that clashed with her purple robe and pink slippers.

She'd asked to see the bone, which was still out back next to the now-sleeping hound dog, and after a brief look, exchanged a glance with Gertie that seemed to convey an entire conversation I wasn't privy to.

"But—" Gertie began.

Ida Belle lifted a hand to cut her off. "Not now. I need to take these rollers out of my hair and get some blood flowing back to my head. Then I'll be able to think clearly."

"Of course," Gertie said.

"Tonight," Ida Belle said and spun around on her pink slippers and exited the lawn by a hedge on the side that she'd walked through earlier.

"What's tonight?" I asked.

"Oh, er...nothing, really. We just meet sometimes—the society ladies, that is."

I studied Gertie for a moment, intrigued by her sudden discomfort. She hadn't seemed the least bit disturbed by the discovery of the bone, and her call to the sheriff had lacked any of the normal drama that would have been present in most people. But a mere glance from a five-foot-two ancient woman, with a slight limp and wearing a bathrobe had her unnerved.

"What exactly do you do at these meetings?"

Gertie's eyes widened. "Oh, the Sinful Ladies Society is a secret society. I can't tell you what we do at meetings."

"Or you'd have to kill me?"

"Ha," Gertie gave a nervous laugh. "Mostly, we knit."

"Uh-huh." Knitting, my foot. I had no idea what was really going on but I could tell Gertie was lying.

"Excuse me," Sheriff Lee interrupted.

I looked over at the sheriff, a shriveled, white-haired man who couldn't have been a day under ninety. "Yes?"

"The water's rising in the bayou—tide's coming in and all—and I'm afraid the bone will wash back into the water."

I stared. "So pick it up."

His eyes widened. "Oh, well, I don't know about that. That's disturbing a crime scene and my deputy needs to document everything."

"The dog chewed on that bone for a good ten minutes. I don't think moving it two feet is going to mess up your evidence."

He stared at me for a while, then looked back at the bone. The bayou level had risen so that it just reached the edge of the bone. It had already submerged the sleeping hound dog in a couple of inches of water, and when I took a closer look, I realized he was blowing bubbles with his partially submerged mouth.

I elbowed Gertie and pointed to the dog. "We should probably wake him up, right? Before he drowns in his sleep."

"Oh, that dog. Do you mind? I'm wearing support hose and you're already barefoot."

I sighed and stepped into the water to shake the dog. Saggy support hose were not something I was interested in seeing in this lifetime, much less today, when my absurdity meter was already on overload.

"Bones," I yelled at the hound as I jostled his body. He let out a loud snore. Not even so much as an eyelid flickered.

"You may have to pick him up," Gertie instructed. "He sleeps like the dead."

"You think?" I gave him one final shake with no result, then straddled him and wrapped my hands underneath his body, hoping if I pulled him to an erect position, he'd wake up and help me out a bit. Just as I was about to lift, he woke up with a start and flipped over, crashing into my right leg and sending me sprawling into the bayou.

Instantly, the suit soaked up a thousand pounds of water and began to itch like crazy. I struggled to rise, but then my legs sank in some sort of quicksand-like mud, and my entire body lowered six inches into the rapidly rising water. And that's when my training kicked in.

In a split second, I shed the heavy suit top, exposing the lacy strip of fabric beneath. I placed the suit top in front of me, flat across the mud and heaved myself onto it with my knees. A short crawl across the suit top put me onto the grass of the backyard, and I collapsed on the lawn, my feet and legs so caked with mud they felt as if they'd been encased in cement. My eyes stung from the water and I clamped them shut, not wanting to think about how much bacteria was running through them.

I heard someone clear their throat and opened one eye. Bones was sitting next to me, clutching the bone in his mouth and looking quite satisfied all the way around. Directly behind him was a pair of blue jean-encased legs. I followed the legs up and found myself looking at the guy I'd seen in town with the monster truck.

"We sorta frown on skinny-dipping around here," he said, "especially at crime scenes."

I jumped up and glared. "This is a...lace-shirt-thingie. I'm hardly naked."

He raised one eyebrow. "Your lace-shirt-thingie is white and thin, so you may as well be."

I looked down and was momentarily horrified to see his assessment was absolutely correct. What in the world were clothes manufacturers thinking, making a top that wasn't water resistant? Girly clothes sucked rocks.

Before I could retort, Gertie slapped her gigantic bag across my chest and glared at him. "Young man, your mother raised you with better manners, and you best just get on with your job or I'll tell her all about this."

He smiled, a slow, sexy smile that you usually see in movies, but he never took his gaze off me. "I *am* doing my job. This is the second time today I've caught this woman breaking the law."

"You're the deputy?"

I don't know why I was surprised. So far, he was the only person in town I'd seen well under the century mark. Given that the sheriff had arrived on horseback, monster-truck guy might be the only person in town that could still function well enough to have a driver's license.

"Carter LeBlanc," he introduced himself. "Protecting the citizens of Sinful."

I pointed to the bone. "You didn't protect that one."

A tiny bit of smug slipped from his expression.

"I'm going to change clothes," I said, "unless, of course, changing clothes in your own home is also a crime in Sinful." I whirled around and started toward the house.

"Only on Wednesdays," Gertie called behind me.

I USED THE WATER HOSE NEXT TO THE BACK PORCH TO WASH the black, gooey mud off my legs and arms. The last thing I wanted to do was track it into the house and have to do something domestic, like mopping, on my first day here. It stuck like tar, and for a moment, I wondered if I was going to need a scraper to get it loose. After what seemed like a lifetime, my skin finally appeared, and I turned off the water and stalked into the house, letting the back door bang behind me.

A quick inspection of the rest of the house's downstairs

didn't reveal a bedroom, so I assumed that meant they were all upstairs. Unless, of course, bedrooms were illegal in Sinful on Saturdays, which was always a possibility. I grabbed the hideous pink luggage and lugged it up the stairs, feeling like I'd been dropped into an alternate universe. I had no idea what I'd expected to find deep in bayou country, but this certainly wasn't it.

I hadn't even been in town one day, and I'd already ruined my shoes, committed two misdemeanor crimes, flashed the deputy, and stumbled upon a potential murder scene. For the first time since I'd left D.C., I was happy that Morrow had insisted on a no-contact rule with him until it was safe to bring me home. If he had any idea that my entrance into Sinful society had been anything other than under the radar, he'd probably fly down here and shoot me himself.

I left the luggage at the top of the stairs and did a quick reconnaissance of the upstairs rooms. The outside of the back of the house didn't contain any structures or trees close enough to the house to make a second-floor window exit possible, but it seemed to have no lighting other than the light next to the back door. The front lawn appeared to be well-lit, and the porch roof provided easy access to the upstairs windows.

I weighed my escape options and finally decided a front-facing room gave me the most flexibility until I could buy some sturdy rope to rappel out of a back window. I knew if Morrow were here he'd be telling me that the likelihood of needing to escape in the middle of the night was slim, but then he'd probably also have told me that inheriting a dog that dug up part of a dead person on my first day in town wasn't probable, either.

The master bedroom was on the front of the house, but staying in a dead woman's room while pretending to be her niece didn't seem right to me, so I selected the other room. It didn't have a connecting bathroom, but then, the desert didn't, either, so traveling to pee was the norm for me. And I had to admit, albeit rather grudgingly, that the other room was rather nice.

It had real wood paneling, hand-carved with ornate designs of inset squares. One wall contained a huge picture window complete with cushioned seat and a built-in bookcase, filled with books, took up another entire wall. It was easy to see what Marge had used this room for. I didn't even like to read, and this room had me ready to select a book and pile up in that window to catch the last of the evening sunlight.

Of course, given the town and the people I'd met so far, likely Marge had a wall full of Bibles or books on knitting. I took a step closer and studied the titles on a shelf, my eyes widening in surprise: *The Study of the Brain, Forensic Investigation Techniques, Eastern Religions, Field Dressing Manual, The Power of Women, A Study of Handguns through the Centuries.*

I glanced at the other shelves, my eyes lingering only long enough to scan some of the titles, and then blinked in amazement. Not a single work of fiction that I could see, and none of the books were what I expected to find in an old spinster woman's house.

I picked up a framed photo sitting at the back of the desk and took a closer look. It was a stocky woman wearing camo and holding a rifle beside an enormous deer. I assumed it was Marge. I put the picture back and shook my head. Apparently Marge and I had more in common than I'd expected. This entire day had been filled with surprises.

Unable to stand the itching from the polyester skirt any longer, I shed my wet garments and tossed one of the pink suitcases on the bed. I'd managed to convince them that librarian-beauty queens also had to mow lawns and take out the trash, so a couple pairs of jeans and several T-shirts were tucked in the corner of the suitcase. I tugged at the jeans that wanted to cling to my damp skin, then pulled on the shirt and reached for the tennis shoes and socks.

Two minutes later, I was beginning to feel almost normal.

A knock sounded on the back door, and a second later, I heard Gertie calling for me. I gathered the wet clothes from the floor and tossed them into the hallway bathroom on my way downstairs. They needed to dry before I could burn them.

Gertie was standing in the kitchen next to Deputy Charming and not looking the least bit pleased. "I tried to tell him to come back later," she said as I entered the kitchen. "A few minutes is hardly enough time for a young lady to make herself presentable."

"That's okay," I said. "I'm not convinced he's worth getting presentable for."

Gertie gave me an approving nod. Deputy Charming was not as amused.

"The personal assessments of criminals rarely interest me," he said, "but I need to ask you a couple of questions before I leave."

I could have argued over the criminal comment, but that would have only kept him in the kitchen longer. "Go ahead," I said. This couldn't possibly take very long as I didn't have anything to tell.

"Did you notice anything odd today?" he asked.

I stared. "Are you kidding? Try everything I've seen since I stepped off the bus. You're going to have to be a *lot* more specific than that."

He sighed. "Since you arrived at the house."

"That really doesn't narrow it down much. But I'll give it a shot and say no because everything I saw that looked odd is apparently business as usual here."

"So you didn't see anyone else along the bayou when you and Gertie went outside?"

Gertie frowned. "I already told you no one was there. I'm old, not blind."

"No one was outside," I confirmed.

"How can you be sure?" he continued to prod. "They may have been hiding."

"Then we wouldn't have seen them, now, would we? But the answer is still no."

"You're sure?" He looked a bit skeptical.

"Look—I have a sixth sense about these things. I can't stand being watched. If someone was out there, I would have known."

He raised his eyebrows. "Seems odd that a beauty queen wouldn't like being watched."

"That was a long time ago. I was in a different place in my life." The understatement of the century.

"Guess that Miss Congeniality title went into the past along with the crown," he said.

"You have no idea. Are we done here? I need a shower and to unpack."

"I'm done for now, but I'll need to know if you're planning on leaving town."

I threw my arms up in the air. "What in the world for? If you knew a single thing about forensics, you'd know that bone has been in the bayou for a while. The only way to get that smooth edging is by the constant flow of running water over time. I hardly sneaked out here years ago, killed a man, and put him in the bayou only to return years later and direct a two-hundred-year-old hound dog to dig up the bone and implicate me."

Gertie stared at me, and I could see the wheels in her mind working. Crap. I'd gone too far with my assessment.

"That's an awful lot of forensic knowledge for a librarian," Deputy Charming said.

Likely, it wouldn't be a good idea to share that I came

about that particular bit of information when I'd stumbled on a mass grave in a river in the Congo and received a rudimentary education from a local scientist.

Librarian. You're a librarian!

"You've probably heard of books," I said. "They tend to collect in libraries. I read. You should try it sometime." I looked over at Gertie. "Thank you for the welcome. Now, if you'll excuse me, I hear a hot shower calling."

I stalked out of the kitchen, not even bothering to take a look back. What the hell was wrong with that man? Was he really so incompetent that he couldn't tell that bone was old? Good Lord, you could literally get away with murder in this town based on the ability of the local law enforcement. Not to mention the sheriff's horse was hardly the optimum choice for a hot pursuit. It looked as old as he was.

Morrow had thought he was doing me a favor sending me to Louisiana, but instead, I was right back in hostile territory, but without the benefit of any training or experience in my environment. As soon as I finished that shower, it was time to break out my laptop and do some reading on Louisiana.

It was stranger than any foreign country I'd ever been in.

CHAPTER FOUR

IT WAS A TEN-MINUTE STRUGGLE TO CUT OFF MOST OF THE length of the fake nails, but I wasn't even going to bother trying typing with those daggers on my fingertips. Who knew acrylic was so hard? It was a fact I stored for future reference. The ability to construct weapons on my body parts might come in handy at some point.

By the time I closed the laptop at midnight, I was more confused than ever. The stories and supposed facts I'd read about Louisiana were wide and varied. The people who lived here couldn't agree on anything—language, how to fish, how to cook—even their legal system wasn't in line with the rest of the United States'.

Apparently, I was just going to have to wing it. The odds of Marge's property becoming a second potential crime scene were unlikely, so I could probably fly below radar from here on out.

I turned off the television on the dresser that had been blaring a late-night marathon of some reality show and crawled into bed. I let out a sigh as my body collapsed on the cushy foam mattress. I'd barely closed my eyes when I popped back upright.

Croak.

What the hell? I reached for my weapon on the nightstand and then cussed when I realized I didn't have a weapon. Sandy-Sue Morrow did not have a license for a handgun and therefore could not check one in airline baggage, much to Director Morrow's delight.

Croak.

I dropped out of bed and crawled over to the window, then slid up the side of the wall and pulled the drapes to the side just enough for me to see outside. The front of the house looked clear, but I knew I wasn't imagining the noise.

Croak.

I whirled around. The noise was coming from the backyard. Where the bayou was. I relaxed a bit and walked into the room across the hall. I peered out the window, but the light above the back door didn't do much to illuminate the backyard.

Croak.

Jesus, it was getting louder!

I replayed the past four hours of Internet research in my mind. Frogs. That had to be it. How in the world did people sleep with all that racket?

Croak.

That did it. I'd seen a shed behind the house during my dog-crime-scene adventure. Surely it contained something that would kill one noisy frog.

The thick, hot, humid air hit me as soon as I stepped out the back door, and I paused for a moment. A wad of toilet paper in my ears would probably work nicely and wouldn't make me sweat.

Croak.

Nope. I wasn't about to live with that for weeks or months

on end, and besides, if I couldn't hear the frog, then I couldn't hear intruders, either. Not an option for the supremely suspicious. I sighed and headed across the lawn to the shed, happy to discover it wasn't locked. I opened the door and peered into the darkness, wishing I'd thought to look for a flashlight in the kitchen. A dim ray of moonlight crept inside, and I finally made out a set of tools hanging on the back wall of the shed. The middle one was a shovel.

Worked for me.

I crept across the backyard toward the bayou, scanning the gently flowing water for my prey.

Croak.

To the left—near the hedge.

As quietly as possible, I traversed the lawn, careful not to step into the bayou water and create a splash. A dark cloud passed over the moon, reducing visibility to almost nothing, and I paused for a moment, hoping the tiny bit of light returned soon. A couple of seconds later, the dim glow of moonlight slid over the water, and I located two humps about two feet from the bank. As the moonlight passed over them, I caught a flash of the white of the eyes before the shadows took over again.

I positioned myself directly in front of the humps and lifted the shovel above my head. But as I began my downward pummel, a hand reached out of the hedges and grabbed the shovel, stopping my swing. An arm hooked around my waist and yanked me a good five feet away from the water before releasing me.

"Coming back to bury the rest of the body?" a deep voice asked.

I let out a sigh. *Deputy Charming.*

And I was standing in the middle of a potential crime scene, at midnight, trying to regain possession of a shovel.

Even with forensics on my side, this had to look a bit suspicious.

"Actually, I was going to kill that frog so I could get some sleep. Do you guys give them amplifiers or something?"

"That's no frog."

"I may not be from here, but I think I know a frog croaking when I hear it."

"Ah, it's a frog making all the noise, but that's not what you were about to hit." He released his grip on the shovel, flipped on a flashlight and shined it on my target. It was two humps of eyes all right, connected to a mouthful of teeth and a long body and tail.

The alligator, apparently resenting the spotlight treatment, spun around in the water faster than I would have thought possible given the length of the creature and disappeared beneath the murky surface.

"Well," I said, not about to let him catch on to the panic that coursed through me at my near miss, "maybe I'll luck out and he'll eat the frog."

He shook his head. "You've got some attitude, lady. I'll give you that."

Suddenly, it occurred to me that I was standing next to a stream of killer-creature-infested water, in the middle of the night, barefoot and wearing my pajamas, a pink, fluffy garment that Harrison had picked out to match the luggage. But that wasn't the part that interested me. I knew why I was there, but why was Deputy Charming there?

"So, you mind telling me exactly what you were doing hiding in the bushes?" I asked.

"Bird watching."

"Bull. You think that person was murdered and someone might come here looking for more pieces."

"I thought it might be interesting to see if anyone turned up here after word about the bone spread around town."

"How can you be so sure it has?"

He laughed. "The Sinful Ladies met tonight at seven. Likely, the entire town knew by eight."

"Uh-huh, and does that nice bunch of little old ladies know you're using them to flush out the guilty party?"

"Ha. Nice bunch of little old ladies. That's a good one." He turned his flashlight across the back lawn toward the street. "Well, since you've likely scared away any of the guilty or the innocent, stalking around in your pajamas and brandishing a shovel, I guess I'll head home."

I stared at his retreating figure as he crossed the yard and disappeared around the front of the house. I had no earthly idea what brand of crazy was being sold in this town, but I was going to make every effort to stay away from it.

Right now, I was going to go back to bed, sleep in until I couldn't sleep any more, and wake up tomorrow pretending this day had never happened. I clutched the shovel with one hand and covered my yawn with the other, my body itching to crawl back on that fabulous mattress.

Croak.

———

I AWAKENED THE NEXT MORNING TO A REPETITIVE DULL thud coming from downstairs. I pulled the cotton balls out of my ears and realized someone was banging on the front door.

At eight a.m.

On a Sunday.

Whoever was assaulting that door was lucky I hadn't been able to travel with my guns, or brought the shovel into the house last night, but that wouldn't stop me from improvising. If they didn't go away quickly, I could probably find something to work with in the kitchen.

I forced myself out of bed, trudged downstairs, and flung

open the front door. A startled Gertie stumbled backward, and I grabbed her just in time to keep her from plummeting backward off the porch.

"Should I even ask what you're doing here this early?" I asked as I stepped back into the house and shuffled to the kitchen to make coffee. I had a feeling this wasn't going to be fast or easy.

"Well, it's Sunday, of course," Gertie said as she trailed behind me. "You're probably just disoriented from the trip and all the excitement yesterday and forgot."

I filled the coffeepot with grounds and water and pressed the switch. "Sunday? Is that supposed to mean something to me?"

Gertie's eyes widened. "Sunday's church day, of course. I know some people think just any old day will do, but 'progressive' isn't appreciated much in southern Louisiana. Unless you're a heathen, you go to church on Sunday."

I opened my mouth to say I was absolutely a heathen and had no desire to attend church, here or anywhere else, but Gertie was on a roll and getting more animated by the second.

"Word of your arrival has spread through town," she continued, "so I knew I had to get over here early before the Catholics got to you."

"Sounds ominous." I poured a cup of coffee and put it in front of Gertie, then poured another for myself. "What exactly do these Catholics do if they 'get to you?'"

"Invite you to their church, of course."

"And that would be bad?"

"It would for me. I'm Baptist. Why, the last time I failed to get to a visitor first and get them into Sinful Baptist, the whole congregation prayed for me every night for a week—out loud. Sinful Catholic sent me a thank-you card. I don't need that kind of embarrassment again."

I cringed. A whole week of praying out loud. No wonder

she was desperate. "I guess it won't kill me to attend, but do they really start this early?"

"Service starts at nine. Used to be eleven, but everything's changed since The Banana Pudding War."

"Was that anything like the Civil War?"

"Oh, much worse," Gertie said, completely serious. "You see, no businesses are open in Sinful on Sundays, because it's a sin to work on the Lord's day and all. But Francine makes the best banana pudding in the parish, so Pastor Don and Father Michael agreed to give Francine's Café special dispensation to be open on Sundays without her having to go to hell."

"So the woman spends her entire Sunday cooking for everyone in town, and all she gets for it is a reprieve from hell? It sounds like she got shortchanged."

Gertie nodded. "You and I agree on that one. Anyway, Francine only has refrigeration for so much food, so she's limited on how much banana pudding she can make."

"Let me guess—there's not enough for everyone in town."

"Nope. Both churches used to start at eleven and run 'til noon, but the Catholics decided to start at ten thirty so they could get out early and ensure their banana pudding. Pastor Don retaliated by starting church at ten, and it went on that way until Mayor Fontleroy made it illegal to start church before nine o'clock or end before ten."

"I'm beginning to understand why this town is called Sinful. Everything is illegal."

"It sometimes seems that way. So you go get dressed, dear. I brought an extra purse big enough to carry your tennis shoes. We'll change during the benediction so that we can sprint to Francine's as soon as Pastor Don says 'amen.'"

"Sounds like a plan."

I didn't have anything to do anyway. Besides, if the banana pudding was worth waging a war and giving someone a free pass on hell, it might be worth checking out. There was also the added bonus of seeing Gertie sprint. Besides, Morrow had told me to blend in with the natives. Apparently, skipping church would draw more attention than my pink luggage.

Even given all the variables, the day had to be less complicated than the one before.

I downed the rest of my coffee and hurried upstairs to find something suitable for God and running. The coolest, thinnest fabric I could find in my assortment of girly wear was a turquoise cotton dress with no sleeves and a skirt that sorta branched out. I figured that would allow air to pass as well as provide plenty of leg room for sprinting, although I doubted the actual need given the apparent median age of the town.

Despite the fact that I was lean and not overly endowed, I tossed on a bra, figuring I'd burst into flames if I walked into church without one. Underwear was a given as you never knew when you might have to go into a fast drop and roll. Flashing people on Main Street was illegal most everywhere. In Sinful, it might get you the death penalty.

I hopped into the bathroom, filled my hands with cold water and splashed it on my face. That was normally the extent of my morning routine, but before I could turn and dash out, I remembered that I was supposed to be acting like a girl. I sighed and walked back into the bedroom to retrieve the bag of makeup I'd left on the desk the night before when I'd unpacked.

As I started to walk back into the bathroom, I saw a woman in the bathroom mirror.

My hand swept to my hip, reaching for the weapon that wasn't there, and a second later, I realized how fortunate that was. The woman in the mirror was me.

I stepped in front of the mirror and turned my head from side to side, watching the long blond extensions bounce across my shoulders. The high, narrow cheekbones that had made me look gaunt with a shaved head now looked exotic. The turquoise dress seemed to make my matching eyes glow, especially with the mass of blond framing it. Good Lord. I was actually pretty.

Like Mom.

The thought ripped through me before I could stop it. I dropped the makeup bag on the floor and clutched the bathroom counter with both hands, staring down at the sink. I hadn't thought about her in years - hadn't allowed myself to. Memories of my mother were the one thing that crippled me, and weakness in my line of work could get you killed.

But I'm not working right now.

That was true, but it didn't mean I shouldn't be on alert. I took a deep breath and shook my head, trying to clear the warring arguments. Gertie was waiting downstairs to take me to church. Thoughts about my mom always led to thoughts of my father. And those thoughts had no place in a church.

I picked the makeup bag up from the floor and pulled out a pale pink lipstick, grabbed my tennis shoes, then hurried out of the room, applying the lipstick as I walked. That was as good as it was getting. I couldn't look at that face—my mother's face—any longer.

"Sleeveless dresses aren't illegal in church, are they?" I asked Gertie as I stepped into the kitchen.

"Heavens, no. We're devout, but we're not barbarians. The humidity here is nothing to sneeze at."

Gertie handed me an enormous tapestry handbag that looked a lot like her own and I dropped tennis shoes and Tic Tacs inside. "Do I need anything else?"

"Looks good to me. If you're ready, let's get going. I want to make sure we get the back pew."

I nodded and followed Gertie outside. I glanced around, but didn't see a vehicle. "We're walking?"

"I had a bit of a fender bender," Gertie said. "Wasn't my fault, of course. It was a really stupid place to put a stop sign."

"Ah," I said, figuring I was better off without the details.

"Anyway, I'm supposed to get my car back this week." Gertie looked over at me. "Marge has a Jeep, you know."

"Really? That's great. I didn't know if I'd have a vehicle while I was here."

Gertie nodded. "The battery's dead because it hasn't been used, but Walter, who owns the general store, ordered one for it last week."

"Cool."

Since Marge's house was only two blocks from Main Street, it didn't take long to arrive at church. I was amused to see that both churches sat on opposite sides of Main Street facing each other—like a religious standoff. I looked down the street and saw the sign for Francine's midway down the block and on the same side as the Catholics.

"They have a bit of a lead," I said, "especially if we have to dodge traffic."

"It's illegal to drive on Main Street when church is letting out."

I rolled my eyes. "Of course it is."

"And horses aren't allowed at all on Sunday, due to the, er... mess. There was the incident with the mayor's wife and a pair of fancy shoes she'd had shipped all the way from France."

I nodded. The sheriff's horse had taken care of business in my backyard the night before. You could lose an entire combat boot in that pile.

Suddenly, I stiffened.

I felt the woman's gaze upon me before I located her, staring at me from across the block. She was probably Gertie's age, had silver hair, and wore a tan pants suit.

Five foot two, one-fifty, possibly born in the past century, a slight limp on the left side.

We stepped off the sidewalk to cross the street to the Baptist church at the same time the other woman stepped off the curb to cross, presumably, to the Catholic church. As we passed in the middle of the street, she shot an amused smile at Gertie and let her handbag slip just enough from her shoulder so that we could see inside.

Gertie sucked in a breath and the other woman's smile broadened as she continued her march to the Catholic church.

"Like getting to wear pants to church isn't enough of an advantage," Gertie said as we entered Sinful Baptist. "Celia Arceneaux's bought the new Nikes. We're doomed."

"Don't worry. I can take her." *Blindfolded and crawling.*

Gertie slid into the back pew and nodded. "I'll let you take the outside seat to get a better jump. As soon as the preacher gets to the 'A' in 'Amen' on the last prayer, you make a break for it."

She dug in her purse and pulled out a pink bottle labeled "cough syrup." She chugged back a good bit, then offered it to me.

"No, thanks," I said. "I'm good."

And not likely to drink out of the same bottle as someone who's sick. Didn't they teach them anything in Sinful?

I glanced around the church and realized no one else was there yet. A quick glance at my watch let me know we had quite a wait before service began. I yawned and then thought about the reason I wasn't all that rested—besides the whole church thing.

"Hey, Gertie, something strange happened last night."

Gertie patted my leg. "I'm sure it seemed that way, but things in Sinful are never quite normal compared to other places."

"No, I mean after all that. I went out at midnight to kill a frog that was keeping me awake, and that deputy was hiding in my bushes."

Gertie frowned but didn't say a word.

"So I got to thinking, given the alligators and hunting accidents and the fact that all this is below sea level and probably floods in a good hurricane, there're at least a hundred valid reasons for a human bone to be in that bayou. But I've got a deputy hiding in the bushes, and that just doesn't say accident, flood, or four-legged predator to me."

"No, I guess it doesn't." She didn't look the least bit happy about it.

"To take that one thought farther, if he thinks a crime has been committed, then that means he must have some guess as to whom that bone belonged."

"I suppose he might," Gertie hedged.

I narrowed my eyes at her and summoned up my limited knowledge of biblical rules. "Are you going to continue to lie by omission? We *are* in church."

Gertie sighed. "I guess not. You're right that plenty of accidents happen in the swamp. Usually, there's a bit of something left behind so we know who the unlucky person was. But about five years ago, Harvey Chicoron disappeared without a trace."

"Did the police look for him?"

Gertie nodded. "And a search party from town combed the swamp. Of course, Carter was still off in the Marine Corps at the time, but he would have heard all about it from his mother. Emmaline has always been a huge gossip."

My self-preservation radar clicked on. Marine Corps, huh? I was going to have to watch my step around Deputy Charming. He was turning out to be more complicated than he appeared. "So, what did everyone think happened to Harvey?"

"Some thought a gator got him and dragged him under with a death roll, so there was nothing left to find. Some thought he ran off with another woman as there was a sizable sum of money transferred to an offshore account around the time he disappeared. He was always cheating on Marie, so running off with another woman wouldn't exactly surprise anyone."

Gertie shook her head. "But mostly, no one cared. Harvey was the meanest, most disagreeable man in Sinful. After the initial surprise at his disappearance wore off, pretty much everyone was just happy he was gone."

"Even Marie?"

"Oh, especially Marie. Her mother had been a tyrant when she was alive, and then she practically sold Marie into indentured servitude with that jackass the way she pressured her to marry him."

Gertie sighed. "And now I've gone and said 'jackass' in church. Five years past and that man still brings out the worst in me."

"I'm sure God knew he was a jackass."

Gertie nodded. "That is a fact. Poor Marie went from living with her mother to being married to Harvey, who was even worse. After he disappeared, Marie actually had the freedom to think and act as she wanted for the first time in all sixty-nine years of her life."

"Sounds like it worked out well all the way around, so then why all the worry? What do you think happened to Harvey?"

"Why, Marie killed him, of course."

CHAPTER FIVE

BEFORE I COULD EVEN FIRE OFF THE HUNDRED OR SO questions that had flashed through my mind, the back doors to the church opened wide and a choir entered, singing. Good grief. Sitting here for an hour was probably going to add another couple hundred questions to the list.

The first of which was exactly why did Gertie think her doormat of a friend had killed her husband? And a close second was, why didn't that thought seem to bother her much? Even the murder of the king of jackasses should have brought a twinge of something—guilt, maybe—to a woman who insisted on being in church every Sunday.

Gertie elbowed me in the ribs and I realized everyone was standing and singing. I sighed and rose along with the rest of the attendees. Civilians were so confusing. The CIA was made up of career agents and ex-military. Everything was structured, and emotion was forbidden during an operation, for good reason. Having a civilian-like emotional moment is exactly what had landed me in church in Sinful, Louisiana, contemplating some doormat of a wife becoming a murderer.

CIA agents didn't share their fears, thoughts or dreams—

assuming they even had any—and they didn't have layers to uncover. If they did, they were so well hidden, they were having a beer with D.B. Cooper. Everything at the CIA was about the work, and while the work itself might be complicated, everything surrounding it was black and white.

Sinful, Louisiana, was so many shades of gray, I was going color-blind.

Once the choir finished their somewhat off-key song, the preacher started talking and my mind faded away from his voice, thinking about my current situation and wondering exactly how long I'd have to stay in Banana Pudding World. Occasionally, the preacher pounded his hand on the pulpit, breaking me out of my thoughts. Finally, he finished dooming everyone to hell, and everyone rose to sing again.

When the preacher started praying right after the song ended, Gertie leaned over and whispered, "Get ready."

I pulled my tennis shoes out of my purse and happily pulled off the heels I'd been wearing. Twenty seconds later, I was ready for action.

"We ask these things in Your name," the preacher said.

"Now," Gertie whispered.

"A—"

I was out the door before the "men" even dropped. The door to the Catholic church flew open as I dashed out into the street, and Gertie's nemesis, Celia, barreled outside. The mid-morning sun hit her straight in the eyes, but she never slowed, running blindly down the sidewalk at a clip much faster than I ever would have imagined.

But it was nothing compared with me.

I could hear Gertie cheering behind me as I lifted the skirt of my dress and leapt over a snow cone stand. I slid a foot or so on the dusty sidewalk, then regained my footing just in time to push open the door to Francine's and bolt inside. Celia huffed in a couple of seconds later and stood there, panting and glaring.

A big woman, probably about fifty, with a ton of blond hair piled on top of her head raised one eyebrow. "Looks like somebody done hired a ringer. You ain't even winded, girl."

"Not a bit," I agreed.

Celia narrowed her eyes at me as Gertie came trotting into the restaurant, the smile on her face as wide as the Grand Canyon.

"Now," Gertie said to Celia, "don't you be giving my friend the stink eye just because you spent all that money on those shoes and you still aren't getting any pudding." She turned to the woman with the hair. "Francine, we'll take a table for eighteen."

"Right this way, Ms. Gertie," Francine said and grabbed a stack of menus.

I followed Francine and Gertie to a stretch of two long tables placed in front of the plate-glass storefront.

"I suppose you'll all be starting with the pudding?" Francine asked.

Gertie nodded and Francine walked through double doors at the back of the seating area, presumably to serve up eighteen orders of banana pudding.

"We're eating dessert first?" I asked.

"Of course not. We're just ordering dessert first so they don't run out. Francine can only fit about twenty-five in her fridge. Celia's got fifteen in her crew."

She looked positively giddy delivering that last statement, and I had to wonder what Celia's crew would have in store for her when they realized the Nikes hadn't done the job. I was, however, interested in seeing how they determined which crew members got the remaining pudding.

Gertie insisted I take the seat at the head of the table, as the "guest of honor."

"Are sixteen more people really coming?" I asked. I hadn't seen Gertie talk to anyone at church.

She nodded. "All the Sinful Ladies will be here shortly."

"Did they skip church?"

Gertie looked horrified. "You can't skip church and then eat out. Why, the whole town would talk about you for a month."

"Don't tell me they're Catholic."

"Heavens, no." Gertie laughed. "The things you come up with. Those of us that don't sing in the choir have church duties. I was let off duties today as I was bringing a guest."

I was just about to ask Gertie about her earlier cryptic comment concerning Marie killing her husband when a shadow fell across the table. I looked up into the frowning face of Deputy LeBlanc. One glance at Gertie told me she wasn't the least bit happy to see him.

"Morning, Ms. Gertie," he said. "How are you today?"

"Fine, thanks," Gertie replied, but she didn't meet his eyes and her lips were drawn in a taut line.

He ignored me completely, which was fine by me.

"You were around when Harvey Chicoron disappeared, right?"

"You know I was."

"They never found any sign of him, right, except for that missing money thing?"

Gertie pursed her lips. "You're the police. I imagine the reports have all the information you can find, and I'm certain you can read as I taught you all four years of high school."

"I've been through the reports, but I wanted to get the local take on the situation."

"He's gone, and no one knows what happened. Not much more to it than that."

"There's always more to it than that. When a person disappears, you should really take a closer look at the person. For example, was he well liked?"

"You know good and well he was the orneriest man in town."

"Hmm. So, no one liked him?"

"You know they didn't."

He raised his eyebrows. "Including Marie?"

Gertie huffed. "I expect Marie had her hands full."

"I don't want to know what you expect. I want to know if Marie liked her husband."

There was dead silence for a long time, and I looked back and forth from Gertie to Deputy LeBlanc. The tension was thicker than the banana pudding Francine slid in front of me, and I couldn't help but notice that as soon as she placed the last bowl on the table, she took off for the kitchen as if there was a fire that needed attending.

"I already said no one liked him," Gertie said finally.

Deputy LeBlanc nodded. "He inherited oil wells from his parents, right? So that means Marie came into quite a comfortable living when he didn't turn up."

"I don't ask people about their finances. It's rude."

He narrowed his eyes at her. "Did she offer the information?"

"No," Gertie snapped at him. "Marie never told me about her finances. Are you satisfied? Because you're ruining my Sunday dinner."

He studied her for a couple of seconds, then nodded. "I'm done for now, but I may be by later after I study those case files again. If I have any more questions, that is."

He looked over at me and nodded. "Ma'am," he said and strolled out of the restaurant.

"What the hell was that about?" I asked. "You could have drowned a herd of elephants in the undercurrent between the two of you."

"He knows I won't lie on Sunday. I tried to dance around the questions, but he still managed to get some information out of me."

I nodded, now understanding Gertie's less-than-direct answers. "So, how much money did Harvey have?"

Gertie cocked her head. "Now, you just heard me say Marie didn't tell me about her finances."

"I know, but I figure someone else did."

She laughed. "It's a good thing Carter isn't as shrewd as you are."

"So you do know?"

"Of course. Marie told Marge and Marge told me and Ida Belle. Harvey sold those oil wells years ago, and his parents owned a ton of real estate, but as soon as he was officially declared dead, Marie got control of everything—all ten and a half million."

"Holy shit!"

Gertie popped me with her napkin. "No biblical cursing on Sundays."

"Ouch," I rubbed the red spot on my forearm. She must have been hell as a high school teacher. "Ten million is a lot of reasons to want a jackass dead. Is that why you think she killed him?"

"That and another reason, but I won't talk about it. I have to discuss it with the society ladies. We have to plan how to handle this before it gets out of control."

She waved a hand toward the window. "Here they come now."

I looked outside and saw a crowd of gray-haired women bearing down on the restaurant.

Sixteen of them, probably from the Jurassic period. Fourteen wearing glasses and seven with hip replacements. Based on skin tone, high blood pressure was running rampant.

"Why don't any of your husbands come to church?" I asked. "Or is that some kind of rule, too?"

Gertie waved a hand in dismissal. "You can't be a member of the Sinful Ladies Society if you have a husband. The original members, like me, are all old maids. We're finally starting to allow widows in, but their husbands have to be dead for at least ten years."

"Why ten years?"

"Seems to take that long to deprogram them from silly man thinking."

"So Marie's not a member?"

"Not yet, but she can petition in another five years."

"If she's not in prison."

"That's not going to happen," Gertie said, and although her voice sounded confident, her expression gave her away completely. Gertie was worried.

Ida Belle plunked down in the chair next to me and gave Gertie a high five. "Good job beating the Catholics to the ringer," she said as she smiled down at the huge bowl of banana pudding on the table in front of her. "I'll bet Celia's kicking herself for buying those expensive shoes."

"If she's not kicking herself now," Gertie said, "she will be later when she looks at that bill and has no banana pudding."

Ida Belle nodded, then looked down the table. "It's time to remember our manners. Everyone, this is Marge Boudreaux's niece. She's the reason you all have banana pudding today, so remember to say a special prayer of thanks for her tonight."

The ladies broke out in a round of enthusiastic applause. Across the café in the corner, Celia and her crew turned to glare.

"What's your name, hon?" one of the little old ladies asked. "I want to make sure I get the right name to God."

"Her name is Sandy-Sue," Ida Belle said.

I cringed and my back stiffened from my butt cheeks all

the way up to my neck. "Actually," I said before I could change my mind, "everyone's always called me Fortune."

"Really?" Gertie said. "Why?"

"Well..." I fidgeted in my chair, trying to think up something that worked besides the truth. Telling them it was short for "soldier of fortune"—due to my mercenary tendencies—probably wouldn't project the right image.

"It's okay, dear," Gertie said. "I don't want to embarrass you."

A light bulb popped on. "That's okay. It was something my mother called me. She used to always say I was going to be worth a fortune someday—you know, with the beauty pageants and such. She really expected me to be an actress or model. I guess the nickname just stuck, and now, I'm not used to answering to anything else."

I was shocked at how easily those lies rolled off my tongue. I hadn't even come close to retching despite the fact that I'd used "beauty pageant," "actress," and "model" in the same delivery. But even more shocking was the ladies' reactions. No one looked even remotely surprised at my expected success based on beauty. They just nodded and smiled like it was the most natural thing in the world.

An optometrist could make a killing in this place.

"How come Francine hasn't brought the list of specials over yet?" Ida Belle asked. "Is she drinking again?"

Ida Belle craned her neck to look over Gertie into the kitchen. Gertie dropped her gaze to the table, not saying a word.

"I don't know anything about the drinking part, although I'm not opposed," I said, "but she probably held back since Deputy LeBlanc was over here grilling Gertie about your friend Marie."

The ladies went instantly quiet and stared at me. I hadn't

commanded this much attention since I'd stolen that drug lord's golden retriever.

"Carter was in here?" Ida Belle asked.

I nodded. "Asking if Marie liked her husband and how much money she inherited—"

Ida Belle's eyes narrowed. "What did you tell him?" she whispered to Gertie.

Gertie paled and bit her lower lip.

"She didn't tell him anything," I volunteered. "She worked around everything except what he already knew, and did a good job of it being that she has that whole lying-on-Sunday rule."

Ida Belle frowned. "Which Carter is well aware of."

"So, is anyone going to tell me exactly what I stepped in the middle of yesterday?" I asked. The more information I could get, the better situated I'd be to avoid the entire mess.

Ida Belle glanced at the other ladies and shook her head. "Now's not the time or place." She lifted her hand to wave at Francine, who hovered in the kitchen doorway. "We're ready when you are, Francine," Ida Belle called out.

The other ladies immediately launched back into the conversations they'd been having before my announcement. Gertie looked over at Ida Belle and opened her mouth to say something, but the tiny shake of Ida Belle's head made her clam right back up.

But was it because of the other ladies or me?

CHAPTER SIX

THE REST OF LUNCH WAS COMPLETELY UNEVENTFUL. ALL OF the ladies split immediately after, claiming knitting, letter writing, and book reading that needed to be done before they returned for evening church service, but I had the sneaking suspicion they might be secretly meeting up to discuss the whole Marie situation.

I was happy to be left out of it all, so I waddled home after consuming chicken-fried steak, mashed potatoes with cream gravy, something called "fried okra," God knows how many dinner rolls, and a big bowl of the best banana pudding I've ever had in my life. Gertie had promptly pointed out that compared with the refrigerated, whipped cream stuff I'd eaten before, it was the *only* banana pudding I'd ever had in my life.

Regardless, I hoped I wouldn't be in Sinful for very long. That sprint from the church to the café in no way covered the calories consumed. In fact, I might have to exercise until October to burn off the calories I'd just taken in. I figured I'd start on Monday.

The Sinful Ladies had been a study in psychology all themselves. Out loud was a lively conversation about the sermon, the pudding, and the latest in fabric down at the general store, but the sideways looks, slight nods, and almost imperceptible shaking of heads belied an entire other conversation happening that I wasn't privy to. I wondered if Gertie had shared her theory about Marie killing her husband with the rest of them. Something must have been said, because the subject of the bone never came up, and in a town as small as Sinful, that had to be the biggest news of the moment.

But what I found the most interesting was that they didn't quiz me on it. I'd expected to be asked to go back to Genesis and talk about my life, and although I'd read all the files, I wondered if my basic knowledge would be enough to satisfy them. They looked completely innocuous, but then, I'd been undercover enough times to know that what you saw on the surface was rarely what went on below.

Something was up in Sinful, Louisiana, and I'd bet my last box of bullets that these ladies were in the fat middle of it. But it wasn't my problem, and I was going to make sure it stayed that way. Below radar. Just like Morrow had insisted.

I spent the rest of the day unpacking the hideous suitcases and getting a lay of the house. Given that Deputy LeBlanc had a penchant for appearing uninvited, I figured burning the suit-cases was probably a bad idea, so I stuck them in a closet in a spare room where at least I didn't have to see them. That chore took only thirty minutes, and then I went to the kitchen to take stock of supplies.

I opened the pantry and stared. Canned goods, dry goods, and preserves filled every shelf, staring back at me in neat rows with every computer-generated label facing directly out. I'd heard about this before with people who'd lived through the Depression, but Marge wasn't quite old enough for that to have been the case. Then I remembered this was hurricane territory. Likely, every pantry in Sinful was fully stocked in case of inclement weather.

I glanced once more at the neatly arranged goods and shook my head before closing the pantry door. Marge either had been really bored one day or had a touch of OCD. I opened the freezer and pulled out the one package inside. It was wrapped in freezer paper and had "Deer steaks" and a date written on it. I had absolutely zero idea how to cook a deer steak, but then I had absolutely zero idea how to cook most things that didn't go in the microwave.

Maybe Marge had a grill tucked away in that storage shed. Otherwise, I was going to have to come up with one or eat canned fruit and vegetables the entire time I was here. There was a pad of paper and pen next to the phone, so I wrote down "meat" on a clean sheet of paper. I wondered briefly if the general store carried packaged meat, or if I was going to have to kill something to get more protein, but I wasn't going to dwell on it just yet.

Even though I'd never killed anything besides a human.

Which was interesting when I thought about it. I supposed for the vast amount of the population, and probably all of the population of Sinful over the age of five, the exact opposite was true. Except, perhaps, for Marie. I frowned when I remembered Gertie's unease with Deputy LeBlanc's questioning and the worry on her face when he walked out of the restaurant. But most of all, I remembered the absolute certainty on her face when she told me that Marie had killed her husband.

He knows I won't lie on Sunday.

I stiffened. Did Gertie know for certain that Harvey had been murdered by his wife or was she just guessing? As much as I was trying to stay out of whatever was bubbling to the surface in Sinful, my thoughts insisted on turning back to that very topic. And if I knew one thing about myself, it was that my instincts were never wrong. Those thoughts were a warning.

I trotted up to the bedroom and grabbed my laptop. It was time for a little more reconnaissance on Sinful, Louisiana, and its residents. I needed to know what I had stepped in the middle of.

Before it blew my cover.

I flopped down on the window seat and leaned back against the pillows propped against the wall. The laptop seemed to take forever to fire up, and I drummed my fingers on the keyboard. Before I launched a full-scale investigation into Sinful, maybe I should see if there was any word from Harrison about my return home. I was supposed to check in with him tonight anyway. Might as well do it now.

Although Morrow had forbidden contact, Harrison had set up a fake email account for me that would make it appear as if he were corresponding with some girl in Idaho whom he met on the Internet. The whole thing sounded icky to me, but Harrison assured me that Internet relationships were the norm these days. It explained a lot about his attachment to his smart phone and aversion to going out in public, but I wisely kept those thoughts to myself, especially as Harrison was breaking protocol to give me updates.

My laptop finally finished booting, and I double-clicked on the icon Harrison had set up to reroute my Internet connection to appear as if it were coming from Idaho. As long as we were careful, there was no reason we'd get caught. I figured if I kept telling myself that, I'd believe it, eventually.

Once the rerouting process completed, I signed into email and saw one message. I rolled my eyes when I saw the return email address. No chance it was spam. This was totally Harrison.

TO: FARMGIRL433@GMAIL.COM
FROM: hotdudeinNE@gmail.com

Hello. Hope things are going well down on the farm. Have you settled into the summer season?

Things are heating up here in NE. I think we're looking at a scorching summer. With any luck, it will begin to cool off early, maybe by the end of August.

Email me when you get a minute.

I FELT MY HEART SINK AS I READ THE SECOND PARAGRAPH. "Things are heating up" meant the situation was getting more critical, but did he mean with Ahmad's organization or inside the CIA with the search for the mole?

I sighed. Either way, he'd made it clear that the soonest he expected positive movement was by the end of August. That left me treading water in Sinful the entire summer.

I clicked Reply and typed in a message.

TO: HOTDUDEINNE@GMAIL.COM
FROM: farmgirl433@gmail.com

I've settled into summer season fine. I'm sorry to hear you're expecting such a hot summer. I always hope for very mild as hot tends to stunt growth and activity, in general. But I guess it's all out of our control.

Are you planning a vacation this year?

I hope to see you soon.

I REREAD THE MESSAGE TO MAKE SURE HE'D GET WHAT I WAS trying to say. The gist of it was that I had arrived safely, wanted to know if he'd be leaving for assignment soon, and hoped to get back to D.C. Soon. The safe arrival part seemed sadly understated given what I'd stepped in the middle of here in Sinful, but the less Harrison knew about it all, the better.

I clicked Send and stared out the window. I don't know what I'd expected to hear in only a day's time, but I couldn't help feeling disappointed. I'd hoped this would be really short-term—like a couple of weeks—and everything would go back to normal. I could have feigned an emergency that sent me back home, and the real Sandy-Sue could hire someone to auction off the contents of the house when she returned from her European vacation. No one would have been the wiser.

Instead, it looked like I was stuck in Sinful, trying to stay out of a murder investigation while attempting to blend with the locals, most of whom were right in the middle of the murder investigation.

———

SUNLIGHT STREAMING DIRECTLY INTO MY EYES AWAKENED me the next morning. I groaned and climbed off the window seat that I'd fallen asleep on the night before. My laptop was on the floor where I'd left it to "rest" my eyes for a minute. They must have been really tired, because a quick check of my watch let me know I'd been asleep in that window seat for six hours.

My mind had probably gone numb from the complete lack of information that I'd found on the citizens of Sinful. I'd dug up exactly five names online—the mayor, the priest, the preacher, a local beauty queen, and someone who'd won a state fair ribbon for the largest squash. The mayor, the priest and the preacher had been listed on a website with information about Louisiana cities. That was all the listing contained aside from the population—253.

The beauty queen had a Facebook page where she apparently spent all day telling the world how much effort it took to be beautiful, what with four-hour hair treatments and eating only negative-fifty calories a day. I'd gotten heartburn just reading it. Facebook had to be the biggest playground for self-absorbed assholes that the world had ever seen.

I'd spent a moment praying she never heard about my arrival in Sinful as she might think we needed to hang out at salons or shop for shoes, and I had been relieved to find that she'd left for Hollywood the year before because she just knew she'd be famous. The fact that the Internet held no other mention of her answered my question about her Hollywood success.

Three hours of searching and all I had was a description of how to tighten the muscles on the inside of my thighs and more makeup tips than Tammy Faye Bakker could have offered. I was really jonesing for my database of information at the CIA. There had to be more to this town than God, banana pudding, and dead things.

The only useful information I'd gleaned was on the alligator. Now, *there* was a worthy opponent. I'd seen one move in the water, and knew I'd be completely outclassed there, but I'd had no idea it could run that fast on land. And besides the underbelly, which it wasn't likely to expose, the kill zone was a quarter-sized spot on the back of its head. I wasn't one to shirk from a challenge, but I'd decided right then and there to keep my distance from water during my stay, which was going to prove a challenge since it was right outside my back door. At the very least, no more night excursions over frogs.

As soon as the stores opened, I was going to see if I could purchase a pair of noise-canceling headphones. It would eliminate my ability to hear intruders, but aside from the dead guy I'd found on my first day, Sinful didn't appear a security threat. Besides, the headphones would solve the nightly problem with my friend the frog, who'd spent the night before running through what I was convinced was an Italian opera. Paper towel wasn't enough to cut the racket.

I threw on jeans and a T-shirt and headed downstairs to let

Bones out for his morning business. At first, I'd been a bit concerned that my stay in Sinful included the care of something living. I couldn't even keep a cactus alive, but Bones was easy. He went outside three times a day, and every evening, he ate a can of soft food. Aside from that, he stayed curled up in the corner, snoring.

Thirty minutes later, I'd polished off coffee, scrambled eggs and toast when I heard someone pounding on my front door. Surely there wasn't church on Monday morning, and I knew of only one person that would be rude enough to bang on my door just before seven a.m. Boy, was he going to get a huge piece of my mind.

I yanked open the front door and yelled, "What the hell do you want now?"

Then I realized that it wasn't Deputy LeBlanc standing on the front porch. Instead, Gertie and Ida Belle stood facing me, eyebrows raised.

"I told you she wasn't a morning person," Gertie said to Ida Belle.

"Well, by God," Ida Belle ranted, "you woke me up and I had to put on my dentures and race out of the house without so much as a cup of coffee. She can darn well let us in and give us something to drink so we can tell her why we're here." Ida Belle narrowed her eyes at me. "Or maybe they'll be more bones found in the bayou."

I wasn't sure if Ida Belle was referring to me or Gertie, but I wasn't taking any chances. Ida Belle could probably take Gertie in a fight, and I really didn't want to have to kill anyone while I was here. I stepped back and waved them inside, figuring whatever had driven Ida Belle out of her house without coffee might be interesting enough to warrant brewing another pot.

Gertie deferred to Ida Belle, who filed in first and marched straight back to the kitchen. She was already pouring herself a cup of coffee by the time Gertie and I got there. She downed the first cup like a shot of whiskey, and I wondered if the inside of her mouth was cauterized. I looked over at Gertie, who gave me an imperceptible shake of her head, and figured it was best not to talk until Ida Belle was done.

She poured herself another cup, then filled one for Gertie and refilled mine and set another pot to brew. I wisely decided to stay out of her way.

"Time to talk turkey," Ida Belle said finally and pointed to the kitchen table.

I grabbed my coffee and slid into a chair at the table. "I don't think I can help you with cooking it or hunting it. I'm strictly a microwave-meal girl."

They both stared at me for a moment; then Gertie's face cleared in understanding and Ida Belle chuckled.

"Not that kind of turkey," Ida Belle said. "The what-the-hell-is-going-on-in-this-town kind of turkey."

"Oh," I said, still cautious. Killing something was often easier than talking. I wasn't out of the woods by a long shot.

"That bone belonged to Harvey," Gertie said.

I choked a bit on my coffee, the million reasons why Gertie sounded so certain of this fact running through my mind. "How exactly do you know that?"

"The DNA test came back early this morning. Myrtle Thibodeaux is Marie's second cousin, and the night dispatch down at the sheriff's department. She's been watching Carter's email, waiting for the results."

"She hacked the deputy's email?"

"Well, I don't think it's really considered hacking when you use your dog's name for your password," Gertie said.

Ida Belle nodded in agreement. "Besides, we can hardly be expected to run this town without information. Deputy LeBlanc is a bit too young to appreciate the order that the

Sinful Ladies have managed for the past fifty years, so he's not on board with keeping us in the loop yet."

"One of your citizens killed her husband and dumped his body in the bayou," I pointed out. "That doesn't sound very orderly."

"It was only a matter of time before someone killed Harvey —a jilted woman, the jilted woman's husband, a business owner he'd ruined—Harvey had all enemies and no friends."

"That part I get," I said, "especially after Gertie called him a jackass in church."

Ida Belle looked at Gertie. "You said 'jackass' in church?" Then she rolled her eyes upward as if looking through the ceiling and directly to Heaven for strength.

"Anyway," I continued, "the disorderly part is not killing Harvey but the disposal of his body. With all the swamp surrounding this town and careful planning, a piece of him should never have washed into my backyard."

Gertie nodded her approval and looked over at Ida Belle. "See. I told you she had a different way of looking at things."

Ida Belle cocked her head to one side and studied me for a bit. "You're sorta direct, aren't you?"

I shrugged because I could be as vague as the next person if the situation merited it. "Maybe."

"Ha." Ida Belle let out a laugh. "I like shrewd. It takes smarts to be good at it." She looked over at Gertie and nodded. "Good call."

"We need your help," Ida Belle said.

"It's a little late to find a better spot to hide the body."

"We know we can't change the past," Ida Belle said. "What we need is a plan to protect Marie."

"Aside from hiring the best attorney possible, I don't know what anyone can do at this point, especially me. Out of curiosity, has anyone asked Marie if she did it? You did say everyone hated him, so why assume it was her?"

"I asked her Saturday evening after I left here," Gertie said, looking slightly ill.

"And?"

Gertie sighed. "She didn't say anything. Her eyes got really big and she sorta squeaked and then ran off inside her house. She hasn't answered the door or her phone since."

"Okay," I said. "Probably not the actions of an innocent person, but it's not exactly hard evidence, either."

Ida Belle nodded. "That's exactly what I was thinking. As long as there's no hard evidence, there's a chance of beating this. Gertie told me about how you knew all that forensic stuff from reading so much at the library, so we figured we'd ask you to help us come up with something to detract suspicion from Marie."

Good Lord. I stretched my mind to all the late-night reruns of *Law & Order* that I'd watched. Somewhere in there had to be an answer, because it wasn't going to come from all those books I'd never read.

"I guess the most logical thing to do is to find another suspect."

Ida Belle nodded. "That creates that unreasonable thing, right?"

"Reasonable doubt?" I asked.

"Yes!" Ida Belle looked pleased. "We need you to find us some reasonable doubt."

"You want me to investigate people so that I can accuse them of murder? What about your secret knitting club? Surely you cooked up something after banana pudding and before evening service."

Gertie shook her head. "Only Ida Belle and I know everything. We're the only two surviving members left of the original five that founded the society. The original five made all the decisions, and it's going to stay that way for now. But we can't investigate the people in Sinful. We have too many preconceived notions about the people here. We need someone from the outside to make the connection, the same way a jury would."

"No way. Even if I had the ability to do such a thing, doesn't it sound rather dangerous to you—getting dirt on people so you can accuse them of murder?"

Ida Belle raised her eyebrows. "Funny, the last thing I would have pegged you for was a coward."

My pulse immediately spiked, and I gripped the coffee mug so tightly the handle snapped and dumped the entire thing on the table. Gertie jumped up to grab a dishrag. Ida Belle just sat there, staring at me across a pool of spilled coffee...challenging me.

Don't get involved.

Morrow's voice echoed in my mind.

I started to shake my head.

The worst kind of person is a coward.

That voice from the grave ripped through me, completely overshadowing Morrow's plea, and twenty years fell away in an instant.

"I'll do it. But I'm going to need information. I'm not going in cold."

Gertie tossed the dishrag on top of the spilled coffee and started clapping. Ida Belle broke out into a smile for the first time that morning.

"We can start with why the bone washed up in my yard. After all this time, why now, and where did it come from?"

"That's the easy part," Gertie said. "It was Edgar that dug it up, and when they flushed the water out of the freshwater pond a couple of weeks ago, it drifted down the bayou until Bones found it."

Ida Belle nodded. "I agree."

"If this Edgar dug it up, why the hell didn't he turn it in?"

Gertie laughed. "Edgar was a hurricane that blew through

here late last year. Flooded the whole area. Couldn't even step off Marge's back porch for over a week or we'd have been right in the bayou. Caught some good bass sitting right there in the wicker chair, though."

Ida Belle nodded. "All sorts of things rose out of the ground during Edgar. Why, my mother's coffin popped straight up out of the grave and cruised down Main Street. I always said you couldn't keep Mother down."

"And your mother always did love Francine's pudding."

I sighed. I was going to need a lot more coffee.

CHAPTER SEVEN

"THE FIRST THING WE NEED IS ANOTHER SUSPECT," I SAID AS I poured one more cup of coffee. "Someone that a jury would believe could have killed Harvey. Juries come with their own prejudices, so we should play to them. Pick a man that's scary looking, slightly odd in behavior, and has more firearms than any one person should need."

Unless they were CIA agents.

Gertie and Ida Belle looked at each other, then back at me.

"Is there a problem?" I asked.

"That describes pretty much every able-bodied man in Sinful," Ida Belle said.

"Seriously?"

"Well," Gertie said, "except for Carter. He's got the firearms, but he's kinda cute, in an aggravating sort of way."

"The aggravating part, I've noticed," I said. "You lost me on the cute."

"Give it some time, honey," Gertie said.

I was just about to tell her I didn't have that much time when someone knocked on my front door.

"Are you expecting anyone?" Gertie asked.

"Who would I be expecting? You're the only people here that I know except—"

Ida Belle sucked in a breath as I stalked out of the kitchen and to the front door.

Deputy LeBlanc stood on my front porch, but rather than wearing his usual semi bored/amused expression, this time he looked angry.

"I need to speak to Gertie and Ida Belle. Are they here?"

I stepped back and waved one hand at the kitchen. This did not look good for the home team.

I hurried behind him as he stomped down the hall and into the kitchen. He stood there in the middle of the room, glaring down at them.

"Where is Marie?"

Their eyes widened.

"At home?" Gertie said.

"No. She's not at home, or I wouldn't be asking, and no one has seen her since Saturday. Tell me where you're hiding her now, and I'll let it all slide."

"But—" Gertie started to reply, but Ida Belle put a hand across her mouth.

"You have got some nerve," Ida Belle said, "marching in here and accusing us of such a thing. And even if Marie isn't at home—even if we knew where she was—explain to me how that's a crime."

"You know darn good and well why it's a crime."

"Actually," I said, "unless Marie is under arrest, it's not a crime to know where she is and not tell you."

He shot me a dirty look. "This is none of your business."

And that pissed me all the way off.

"You're threatening my guests in my house," I said. "So unless you're planning on arresting someone, I want you to get out."

"You're making a big mistake," he said. "Whatever these two are up to, you don't want any part of it."

"All they're 'up to' is a cup of coffee." I waved toward the front of the house.

Deputy LeBlanc shot one more look of warning at Gertie and Ida Belle and left, slamming the front door behind him.

"Oh my God—" Gertie started.

"What the hell—" Ida Belle chimed in.

"Hold up!" I interrupted before they got too wound up. "Do those looks of absolute consternation and confusion mean neither of you knew Marie was missing?"

"We had no idea," Gertie said. "I swear it. I mean, she wasn't at church on Sunday, but we figured with the bone being found and all, she was just lying low."

"This is not good," Ida Belle said.

"No shit, it's not good," I agreed. "It makes her look guilty as hell."

"Well...," Gertie said.

I waved a hand in aggravation. "The fact that she probably *is* guilty is not the point. The point is that it does no good to divert suspicion to someone else if Marie is running around practically waving banners that say 'I did it.'"

"I agree this is not optimal," Ida Belle said.

"Not optimal?" I stared. "It's a friggin' disaster. Do either of you have any idea where she might have gone?"

They both shook their heads.

I felt my exasperation rise and cursed my father for ingraining the coward challenge in my psyche. My helping Ida Belle and Gertie was all his fault, and not at all what I'd signed up for when I agreed to come here. Knitting would have been a breeze compared with this. I took a deep breath and tried to remind myself that they were old and their only life experience was this God-forsaken town. I needed to do the difficult thinking.

"Okay," I said, "if Marie was in trouble, who would she call?"

"Probably not her daughter," Gertie said. "She lives out of state and Marie wouldn't want to worry her. And with her cousin working for the sheriff, well, she could hardly get her involved."

Ida Belle nodded. "She's right. Marie doesn't have much family. The only people she would have called outside of those two is me or Gertie, and you have my word, neither one of us has heard from her since Gertie talked to her on Saturday."

"Well, it is pointless to continue finding suspects until we locate Marie and get her to stop drawing attention to herself. I can come up with some sort of story for her to tell about her disappearance, but it won't do any good unless we can get Marie back here to tell it."

"Harvey had that camp out on Number Two," Gertie said. "Do you think she went there?"

"Number Two?"

"It's an island out in the swamp north of here," Ida Belle said. "It's called Number Two Island because the whole place has a rather foul smell."

"And people intentionally go there? Pitch tents there and camp?"

"Not a tent camp," Ida Belle said. "Camps are buildings—probably closest to a cabin."

"The fishing is great on Number Two," Gertie said. "Just dab a little Mentholatum in your nostrils and you're good for several hours."

"I'll pass." In no way, shape, or form did my helping them have to include traipsing around in the swamp on a stinky island that was probably surrounded by my only local predatory equal, the alligator.

"You can't pass," Gertie said. "Even if we find Marie, we'll never be able to convince her to return to Sinful unless she meets you. You're our ace in the hole."

"That's interesting, considering I just arrived two days ago. What would you have done to help Marie if I hadn't come to town?"

"I hear Brazil is nice this time of year," Gertie said.

I sighed. And it probably didn't smell like crap.

———

IDA BELLE INSISTED THAT I HAD NOTHING SUITABLE TO wear to Number Two and that a trip to the general store was in order. I spent a very scary half mile clutching the back door handle of Gertie's Cadillac while she herded the monstrous sedan down the center of the street. Other vehicles pulled onto curbs and into driveways to avoid her.

"Damn it, Gertie," Ida Belle complained from the passenger's seat. "You're driving without your glasses again. You're going to kill someone."

Like me.

"I've got on my glasses," Gertie said.

"You've got on your reading glasses."

"All I need is reading glasses."

"That's not what Dr. Morgan said."

Gertie frowned. "What the heck does he know? I changed the man's diapers, and now he's telling me I have old eyes. Well, I'm not having any of it. My eyes were perfectly fine for reading until he convinced me to wear reading glasses. Now I can't even read the label on canned goods without having these things on."

Ida Belle looked back at me and rolled her eyes. "Yeah, I'm sure that's it—the *glasses* are making your vision worse."

Finally, we pulled up at the curb of the general store, and I breathed a sigh of relief as I strolled inside. I hoped Gertie wasn't doing the boat driving, too. An older, stocky man at a counter at the back of the store greeted me as I walked inside.

"Welcome," he said. "You must be Marge's niece. I'm Walter and this is my store."

Six foot one. Two hundred fifty-six pounds. Good vision but high cholesterol.

"Nice to meet you, Walter," I said.

He nodded. "I've been putting together some supplies for you."

I looked back at Gertie and Ida Belle, who shook their heads.

"What kind of supplies?"

He pulled a pair of silencing headphones from beneath the cabinet and set them on the counter. "Had to dig through storage to find these. Not much call for silencing with Sinful hunters, but I had one pair anyway. They're a little dusty, but good quality."

He bent over and picked up a cardboard box and set it on the counter. "That should be everything you need for today."

I peered in the box and saw hip waders, work gloves, camouflage pants and T-shirt, rope, a hunting knife, and a rifle.

I looked up at him. "I like you."

Walter laughed and shot a look at Ida Belle. "If only all females were so easy to please. Technically, the rifle is one Ida Belle ordered, but I figured she wouldn't mind the loan."

Ida Belle marched up to the counter and glared at Walter. "I demand to know who gave you information on this young woman."

I looked at Walter, who winked at me. "My guess," I said, "is he's been talking to Deputy LeBlanc."

"Yep," Walter said. "Came in here yesterday laughing over your issue with the frogs, but he wasn't laughing today. Came in here mad as heck over Marie being missing."

"Saw that myself this morning," I said.

"Well, I figured since Marie is missing and Ida Belle and Gertie was at your house darned near before coffee time that they was roping you into helping them with some nonsense. Since Harvey had that camp over on Number Two, I figured that's where they'd want you to go look with them."

He pulled a tab from the cash register drawer and handed it to Ida Belle. "I put everything but the headphones on your tab as I figure that stuff is for Sinful Ladies' business. I gassed up my boat and docked it around back. Put a tank of gas on your tab as well."

He handed a second tab to me. "That's for the headphones. Just sign and we can settle up later when you come back for more supplies. You'll want to get out to Number Two before the breeze picks up. I'm throwing in some Mentholatum for free, just 'cause I feel sorry for you."

I put the headphones in the box with the rest of the supplies. "I feel sorry for me, too."

I followed Ida Belle and Gertie out the back entrance of the store and down to the boat dock.

"Darn man has always had a smart mouth on him," Ida Belle complained.

"Well, you *have* turned down his marriage proposals for over forty years," Gertie said. "He was bound to get testy about it sooner or later."

Forty years! I didn't have that kind of interest or dedication to anything.

"Walter knows good and well I'm not about to have a man around twenty-four/seven trying to tell me what to do. If he hasn't processed 'no' in forty years, then it's his own fault."

I eyeballed the tiny scrap of floating aluminum and hoped like hell there were life vests available. "Um, who exactly is driving the boat?"

"I am," Ida Belle said.

Gertie started to protest, and Ida Belle held a hand up to stop her.

"Don't even go there," Ida Belle said. "When you bring your glasses, I'll consider riding with you again, but not a minute before."

Gertie crossed her arms over her chest. "Then I guess you'll be walking to the meeting tonight."

"Me and my corns will manage the two blocks just fine." Ida Belle looked over at me. "That equipment isn't doing you any good in the box. Go back in the store and change clothes. And get a move on. The bouquet of Number Two tends to rise with the temperature."

Great.

I trudged back to the store wondering what in the world I'd done to deserve all this. Then I remembered that I'd killed the brother of an arms dealer with a stiletto and everything made sense again. If this was the way karmic justice worked, I was going to make darn sure I didn't kill the wrong person in the future.

"Changing room is on the left," Walter called out, not even looking up from his newspaper as I walked inside the store.

I located the changing room and pulled on the camouflage pants, T-shirt and hip waders, then turned to look at myself in the mirror. It was the most ridiculous thing I'd seen in my life. The hip waders bloused out like a clown suit, complete with camo suspenders. All I needed was a litter of Chihuahuas to carry around in there and I'd be ready for a second career option.

I walked out of the dressing room and up to the counter. Walter lowered his paper and gave me the once-over, then shook his head.

"Is this really the best thing to wear into the swamp?" I asked. "Can't I just wear jeans and rubber boots?"

"Some places in the swamp are like quicksand. Looks like

ground—then you step on it and sink a good three feet in the mud. If you was to wear the boots, you wouldn't make it ten feet before one was stuck in a mud pit and long gone. For you to lose them waders, you'd have to step in something up to your waist."

"I'm not going to need to run or anything, am I? Because these things really restrict movement."

Walter's brow scrunched together for a couple of seconds, then he shook his head. "I suppose a rogue gator is always a possibility. But given as how I already heard about your sprint to Francine's yesterday, I'm betting money you'll be faster than Ida Belle or Gertie. A gator can't eat all of you, so from your perspective, running's not really a worry."

I stared at him, certain he was joking, but he merely lifted his paper and went back to reading the cartoons. Jeez. And I thought I was ruthless. Maybe he was angrier over Ida Belle turning down those marriage proposals than she imagined.

I hefted my supply box up on the counter. "Can I leave everything I don't need right now and pick it up when we get back?"

"Sure. I'll just put it behind the counter."

"I don't suppose you have some mirrored sunglasses, do you?"

"Yep. Most people going on the water prefer polarized, though."

"I'm not planning on spending much time on the water, so mirrored are fine." And allowed you to closely watch other people without them realizing what you were doing.

Walter rummaged through a drawer behind the counter and pulled out a pair of sunglasses. I stuck them on top of my head, then dug through the box, stuffing things I thought I might need into the camo pants pockets. I started to load the rifle, then stopped.

"I really appreciate you including Ida Belle's rifle in the

gear," I said, "but if I have to fire while running, a handgun would work better."

Walter lowered his paper and stared at me, raising one eyebrow. "You been watching them cop shows on television?"

"Maybe?" I replied, hoping it would cover my faux pas of asking for weaponry that a librarian probably shouldn't have the ability to use.

He narrowed his eyes at me, and I worried for a moment that I'd taken things too far.

"What's a pretty young thing like you know about shooting a handgun?"

"Pretty young things who live in big cities can't shop after dark without protection."

He stared a couple of seconds longer, and I kept my gaze steady. Finally, he sighed and pulled a pistol from underneath the counter.

"I have to run a background check on you to sell you a pistol," he said. "There's no way I can get that check done in the next ten minutes, so seeing as you're Marge's family, I'm going to loan you my gun. But if you lose it, or shoot anything but a gator with it, I'm going to swear you stole it."

"Sounds like a plan," I said as I put the rifle back in my supplies box and took the pistol from him. "I take it you know this Number Two?"

"Yep. Got a fishing camp out there."

"Is there anything in particular I should watch out for?"

He snorted. "Yeah. You're riding in the boat with 'em."

I shoved the pistol in my camo pants and left the store before I changed my mind. I was way too close to agreeing with him.

Ida Belle was perched at the back of a tiny aluminum boat next to an outboard motor. Gertie sat on a bench in the middle, wearing a life vest and squinting at me as I approached the bank.

"Couldn't we borrow a bigger boat?" I asked.

"A bigger boat won't fit down the channel," Ida Belle said.

"Are you sure this thing's safe?"

Ida Belle waved a hand in exasperation. "Just get in and sit down up front. Unless you plan on dancing in here, the thing's fine. And push me away from the bank, will you?"

I looked at the wobbly piece of tin and hesitated, then chastised myself. I'd seen plenty of boat launches on movies. I could handle this.

I untied the boat from a giant post, then pushed the front of the boat just a bit with my foot. The mud it was resting in must have been slick because the boat launched backward. Panicked, I leapt from the bank onto the flat shelf on the front of the boat, waders and all, and froze in a judo fighting stance.

Gertie clapped, grinning from ear to ear. "That was amazing. I figured you were going to flip over into the bayou, and then we'd have to fish you out and buy you new waders."

Great. Twenty-five years of martial arts training had managed to entertain Mother Time in the bayou. My father would be proud.

"I thought the waders were waterproof," I said. "Why would you have to replace them if I fell in?"

"They're water*tight*," Ida Belle said. "So as soon as you get in water over the waistline, they'll fill up and you'll sink like a stone. If that happens, you have to shed those waders and let them go. Then you'll have to buy another set."

"That happen a lot?"

"Probably more than you want to know about."

"Hmmmm."

"Are you going to sit down?" Ida Belle asked. "Or am I supposed to drive down the bayou with you up there looking like a Jackie Chan hood ornament?"

I hopped down into the boat and sat on the bench at the

front. It was a good thing I did. Next thing I knew, Ida Belle twisted the throttle on the boat motor and it launched a good two inches out of the water and ten feet forward in less than a second. If my feet hadn't been firmly planted on the bottom of the boat, I would have been face-first in the aluminum.

Gertie, however, did not fare as well. She flipped over backward off the bench, still clutching the shotgun, and shot out the lights on Walter's pier. I looked back at the store to find Walter standing at the back door, shaking his head.

"I'm putting that on your tab," he yelled as Ida Belle powered the boat away from the store.

I hoped Ida Belle had rich parents or had retired from a lucrative career. Otherwise, she might have to take Walter up on his proposal in order to clear her tab.

I rose and staggered the couple of steps to the bench to take the shotgun from Gertie, then helped her back onto the bench. "I'll just hold on to this," I said, nodding at the shotgun.

"It had already been pumped." Gertie said and frowned at Ida Belle. "Who leaves their shotgun pumped?"

"I do," Ida Belle said. "I sprained my wrist last week, and it's delayed my response time."

Gertie's frown cleared. "Well, why didn't you say so?"

I was beginning to see the validity in Walter's warning.

"So, how far is it to Number Two?"

"Shouldn't take more than twenty minutes with the bayou this smooth," Ida Belle said as the boat slammed over a wave, jarring my teeth.

"And Harvey's camp is on the bank?" Please. Please. Please.

"Not right now. The tide's out, so the water level will be too low to pull all the way up to his pier. We'll have about a quarter-mile walk to get around to it."

I didn't even bother to hold in the sigh. It felt like an entire day had already passed, and yet we still had to walk in sludge, find Marie, convince her to return to Sinful, drag her back if she didn't want to go, come up with a reasonable explanation for her disappearance to Number Two, and find someone else to blame for Harvey's death.

I'd disabled a nuclear warhead with less effort.

CHAPTER EIGHT

I SMELLED NUMBER TWO BEFORE I SAW IT. I'D LIKE TO SAY that's because I was facing backward in the boat, but the reality is, the aroma of N2 wafted across my nose before we'd even rounded the narrow channel to get a clear view.

I blanched and saw Gertie pull the Mentholatum from her pocket. I remembered Walter had given me some and pulled the container from one of my camo pants pockets. I swiped my finger in the gel and dabbed a bit in my nostrils, then inhaled a little.

And almost passed out.

Ida Belle rounded a corner, and I turned around to see what in the world could create such a stench. I was appalled to see an island of mud and cypress trees about a hundred yards away across a small lake, filled with stumps. There wasn't a breath of air, which meant that stench was literally permeating over a hundred yards away from the source. Ida Belle cut the boat speed down to almost nothing and began to weave in and out of the stumps.

I was beginning to see the wisdom of Marie hiding out

there. No one in their right mind would want to set foot on the place.

I dipped my finger in the Mentholatum again, this time pulling up a wad of the gel, and shoved the entire thing into my nostrils. I sniffed again to test, then drove my entire nose into the bottle.

"It isn't usually this bad," Gertie said.

"Why is it this bad now?"

"Because it's summer. Heat tends to ripen the aroma. No one comes here much until cooler weather. The speckled trout are huge."

"I don't care if the fish are covered in gold. I wouldn't come here ever."

"If you'd been to one of our all-night fish fries after a day on Number Two, you'd change your mind," Gertie said.

"Not unless you had a mind-numbing amount of beer, I wouldn't."

Ida Belle snorted. "Of course there's beer. Who has a fish fry without beer?"

I raised my eyebrows at her. "Southern Baptists?"

Ida Belle waved a hand in dismissal. "That's only in front of other people. The Sinful Ladies don't count."

Gertie nodded and smiled. "Do you know why you always take two Baptists fishing?"

"I have no idea."

"Because if you take only one, he'll drink all the beer." She laughed so hard, she doubled over on the bench.

Ida Belle rolled her eyes. "That joke is as old as Gertie, but it never ceases to tickle her."

"So, let me get this straight," I said. "You have all these religious rules, like no drinking, but you only observe them in front of other people?"

"Yeah, that pretty much sums it up," Ida Belle said.

"But doesn't God see it?"

"Oh hell," Ida Belle said. "God doesn't care about drinking beer. All those rules were made up by people trying to prevent you from doing something really wrong. Drunks make stupid decisions. If you don't drink, there's less chance of doing something stupid."

I saw her point in a very broad way, but as I'd managed to do plenty of stupid things completely sober—this exact moment being one of them—I decided to let the whole thing drop. Religion was by and large constructed by men, and I had yet to find a man who was logical. Deconstructing religious rules would definitely be a journey into madness.

"Almost there," Ida Belle said. "Fortune, grab that pylon at the dock and pull us alongside where the ladder is."

I turned around and almost got a face full of wood. If I hadn't had the reflexes of a trained killer, that's exactly what would have happened. Instead, I threw my hands up in front of my face and pressed them against the pylon. When the boat came to a stop, I reached for the rope and tied the boat off to the dock.

"Good job." Ida Belle nodded approvingly.

"A little more notice would have been nice," I replied.

"Bah. I'm keeping you on your toes. You never know when you might have to move fast out here. Doesn't do any good to get complacent."

"Trust me, I plan on moving at the speed of light out here." I started up the ladder and got the top of my hip waders caught on a loose board. Ida Belle and Gertie just stood there, watching me struggle with the rubbery material and the piece of rotten wood until I finally wrenched the entire piece from the dock.

"Okay, maybe the speed of sound," I said as I climbed onto the dock.

"Maybe we should have told her there was a bowl of banana pudding on the other side of the island," Gertie said.

I reached down to grab the shotgun Gertie handed me, not even bothering to argue. I hadn't run down Main Street yesterday for banana pudding. Until yesterday, I didn't even know what real banana pudding was. I'd run down Main Street because I couldn't stand walking away from a challenge. All I cared about was finishing first. The pudding had turned out to be the icing on top, but it wasn't the reason I'd carried tennis shoes into church.

I put the shotgun on the deck and went to extend my hand to Gertie, but found she was already stepping onto the deck, with Ida Belle close behind. Apparently, they were schooled in the fine art of hip-wader climbing. I consoled myself by thinking I'd probably made it easier for them by removing that rotten piece of wood.

Before I could make a move for the shotgun, Gertie swiped it up and gave me a look that said she wasn't going to part with it easily. I wasn't about to get in a wrestling match with an old woman carrying a loaded weapon, especially on an island of dung. With my luck, she'd shoot a hole in the boat and we'd be stuck here.

"Where to now?" I asked.

Ida Belle pointed off to the left. "That way. The camp's right on the water...well, when there's water. We can follow the bank right up to the front door."

I nodded and stepped off the deck and into the same inky goo that was in the bayou behind my house. I yanked my leg out of the goo and plodded up to more firm ground. Ida Belle trudged through the sludge and stepped past me down the left bank. I waited for Gertie to fall in line behind her and then picked up the tail.

"So, what happens if Marie doesn't want to leave?" I asked as we walked.

"That's not an option," Ida Belle said, the tone of her voice leaving no doubt in my mind just how serious she was.

"What if she's not here?"

"Where else would she be? Harvey's boat is gone. I seriously doubt she's gone offshore fishing, especially as she doesn't even eat fish."

"You didn't tell me Harvey's boat was gone."

"We didn't think to check until after Carter barged into your house this morning. Gertie called one of the Sinful Ladies, and she checked while you were getting ready to leave your house."

"So, if Marie took the boat and came here, then why wasn't it at the dock?"

"She probably drove it around the other side of the island where the brush is denser and hid it close to the bank."

"That sounds pretty sharp for a doormat housewife."

"We might have taught her a few things over the years," Gertie said. "Just in case."

"In case she murdered her husband and needed to hide?"

"No! Lord, the things you come up with. In case he was being particularly mean and she needed to get away for a while. Harvey was too stupid and lazy to have looked for a hidden boat. He would have checked the dock and assumed she wasn't there. The only thing the man ever put energy into was chasing other women."

"So why didn't Marie leave him?"

"The money, of course. Marie didn't have what you'd call marketable skills, and her own parents had been poor as church mice. The prenuptial Harvey's family had her sign was airtight. If she left, it would be with the clothes on her back and that was it."

"But surely you guys would have helped her."

"Of course, and don't think we didn't offer a million times, some of us more stringently than others. But Marie wouldn't hear of it because of Charlie."

"Who's Charlie?"

"Her brother," Gertie piped in. "He was a surprise baby for her mother, so much younger than Marie. Back when I was a girl, we would have called Charlie 'slow.' Of course we know now that he's got autism. He's fairly high functioning after training, but until Marie got him into therapy and the group home where specialists worked with him, he had a pretty meager existence."

I frowned, beginning to get the picture. "And Marie was footing the bill for Charlie's therapy and living expenses."

"Of course. Marie loves that boy more than anything in the world. Can't blame her, really. He's just as sweet as he can be. But all those doctors aren't cheap, and none of us could afford to keep up with his care. We're comfortable, but we're not millionaires like Harvey."

I blew out a breath. If Marie was convicted of murdering Harvey, the courts would probably award the inheritance to his nearest living relatives.

I'd felt bad enough for Marie just knowing her husband abused her, but knowing she didn't have another option—not a financially viable one anyway—cranked up my empathy to a place it had never been. She'd stayed all those years with a butthole to take care of her autistic brother. That was the kind of thing made-for-TV movies focused on.

The woman was a hero, not a villain. From here on out, I'd stop complaining about helping Ida Belle and Gertie, who clearly had their hearts in the right place. If it meant Marie didn't go to prison, it would be worth the hassle and definitely a more worthwhile project than packing up the belongings of a dead woman whom I was supposed to be related to.

I glanced down at my watch. Almost fifteen minutes had passed. We had to be close. And just as that thought left my mind, we rounded a corner and there was the camp.

It looked rather fancy for a camp, based on my experience in the desert, but I supposed it was too run down and slapped together to rate calling it a lake house. "Shack from a horror movie" was the best description I could come up with. The wood sides were weathered and warped in some places. The tin roof had holes rusted completely through in several areas. Good thing there hadn't been a storm or Marie would have been swimming in there.

We walked to the front door, which was constructed - badly - from a sheet of plywood. Although no sound came from inside, and I was fairly certain that Marie was not a bad person, my hand still hovered over my waistband as Ida Belle pushed open the door.

"It's empty," she said, sounding defeated.

Instantly, I relaxed my arm and dropped it at my side. Ida Belle stepped into the camp with me and Gertie in tow. The inside was just as run-down as the outside. A lopsided, wooden table stood in one corner, covered with chipped dishes and a Coleman stove. A cot piled high with rumpled blankets stood in the corner opposite the table. Makeshift shelves on the wall above the table contained boxes of dry food and cans of beans and corn. The floor was a mixture of dirt and trash.

"It looks abandoned," I said.

"It pretty much has been," Ida Belle said. "Marie never liked fishing."

"You guys just leave food sitting out at these places year-round?"

"Most people leave some staples. Things that won't spoil."

"What about animals? This shack is hardly secure. Don't animals get in and eat things?"

Ida Belle shook her head. "There aren't any animals on Number Two. Even birds don't land here."

I held in a sigh. Typical human shortsightedness. Animals wouldn't come near the place, so people thought it would be a good place to set up shop.

"Well, ladies," I said. "It looks like this was a bust. Clearly, Marie's not here."

"Ida Belle frowned. "No, but she was recently."

I spun around to look at her. "How do you know that?"

"Because those blankets aren't filthy like everything else in here."

I lifted one of the blankets from the cot and smelled it. Sure enough, I got a nose full of fabric softener and Mentholatum.

"Would she have gone anywhere else on the island?"

"It's not like it's Hawaii or something," Ida Belle said. "There's nothing more out here than what's right here—run-down camps, mud and cypress trees."

"Maybe she heard us coming and ran," Gertie suggested.

I stepped back outside and cased the outside of the shack. "The only prints I see are the ones we made getting here. So unless Marie can fly, she left long enough ago for the mud to fill in her tracks."

Ida Belle nodded. "Which means before high tide. The last would have been about eight hours ago."

"Well, I don't think she would have left in the middle of the night," I said, "so it's probably safe to say she left before last night."

"Probably so," Ida Belle agreed.

"Then where is she now? The two of you have got to have more ideas than this stretch of stinking mud."

Gertie turned up her hands. "We don't have a clue."

"None of you? All that strength and power you keep claiming the Sinful Ladies Society has, and not a one of you has an idea where Marie is?"

Gertie shook her head. "We already told you that we didn't fill the other ladies in on this. We were trying to keep it quiet."

I narrowed my eyes at them. "So I'm supposed to believe

you were knitting at that Saturday-night meeting—just like you claimed to be on Sunday after church."

"We *were* knitting on Sunday," Gertie said.

"But not on Saturday night?"

The guilty expression gave Gertie away completely. Ida Belle shot one look at Gertie and sighed.

"Don't ever commit a murder," Ida Belle said to Gertie. "Everyone would know it was you in a heartbeat."

"I knew it. You *weren't* knitting on Saturday night."

"No." Ida Belle said.

"So, what were you doing that was such a secret?"

"Making moonshine."

I stared. "You're kidding me."

"Nope."

"Moonshine? As in rednecks and brown jugs and prohibition?"

Ida Belle drew herself up straight. "It hasn't been illegal in quite some time. We're hardly rednecks, and we put all of our moonshine into pretty pink cough syrup bottles."

My mind flashed back to Gertie chugging cough syrup before service on Sunday.

"You were stoned at church?" I asked.

"Of course not," Gertie said. "You only have a little cough syrup before church to take the edge off Pastor Don's boring sermons and that choir that manages to sing everything off-key. It's not like we're on the toot."

"And what exactly does the pastor think about you drinking cough syrup at church?"

"He thinks it keeps us from coughing, I guess." Ida Belle narrowed her eyes at me. "Do you really think all those women in western days had all those cramps and headaches and such? But they all carried around laudanum. You know why— because the menfolk didn't think anything of it."

"But none of you are married."

Gertie brightened up. "Oh, we sell it every year at the church bazaar. Probably every woman in Sinful has a case or two. It's made the most money of all the offerings ten years running. Even more than Francine's banana pudding."

Ida Belle nodded. "The rate of divorce in Sinful dropped twenty percent when we started selling the cough syrup."

I took a final look at the shack and shook my head. "Maybe you should have given Marie a double dose."

CHAPTER NINE

THE WALK BACK TO THE DOCK SEEMED TWICE AS LONG AS the walk to the shack. Granted, the stench was growing worse with every degree that the temperature increased, but I don't think that was what made it drag.

Gertie and Ida Belle were worried. Seriously worried. They'd tried to hide it in stories about moonshine, probably figuring it would distract me from the anxious glances and fidgeting that had gone on in the shack, but I'd noticed. I noticed everything people did. It was a hazard of my profession.

Things were looking worse and worse for Marie, and at this point, I didn't have a single idea to offer up.

We were walking single file back to the dock, except this time I was walking up front, while Gertie and Ida Belle lagged behind. I could hear their low whispers as I trudged along the bank, but I didn't even try to listen. This whole situation was shaping up to a murder trial, and the last thing I needed was to be in the middle of that fiasco. It was probably better if my knowledge of the situation ended here.

I rounded the last corner and started across the remaining

twenty yards to the dock. When I stepped up on the dock, I turned around to offer a hand to help up Gertie and Ida Belle. They were about twenty feet behind me, Ida Belle frowning and Gertie looking so worried it made me feel bad all over again about the entire mess.

I'd barely tuned in to the faint rustle of marsh grass on the far side of the clearing when the alligator rushed out of the brush behind Ida Belle and Gertie, moving faster than I would have believed possible. I yelled and reached for my weapon, but before I could even wrangle it out of my waders, Ida Belle shoved Gertie out of the path of the charging monster, spun away from him, pulled her pistol, and fired, planting a bullet right in that quarter-sized kill spot on the back of his head.

The ten-foot beast slumped to the ground, his jaws still open.

"Holy shit!" I cried and ran over to help a dazed Gertie up from the ground.

I looked over at Ida Belle, who was calmly holstering the pistol at her waist. "If I hadn't seen that, I wouldn't believe it."

Ida Belle shrugged. "You plan on tromping through the bayou your whole life, there's certain skills you need to develop."

"Are you kidding me? I've met s—um, big game hunters that couldn't make that shot." I held in a sigh of relief that I'd managed to catch myself before saying "snipers." Likely, beauty queen-librarians didn't meet many snipers, at least, not that they were aware of.

I looked over at Gertie, trying to figure out if Ida Belle was joking with me. Maybe she was in shock. Maybe she'd been afraid they were going to die, had pulled off the luckiest shot in the world, but didn't want to scare Gertie by saying it.

"Is she serious?" I muttered to Gertie.

Ida Belle walked past me, all nonchalant, stepped on the

dock, and untied the boat. "My daddy taught me to shoot," she said. "He was a harsh taskmaster."

I felt a sharp pain in my chest. "Yeah, I get that."

"I thought your father died when you were a kid?" Gertie asked.

"He did, but his disapproval still lingers on."

Gertie shot a look at Ida Belle, who had jumped in the boat and was messing with the motor, studiously avoiding the entire conversation. "Ida Belle's father was a hard man. He wanted sons, you see, but Ida Belle's mother had complications when giving birth to her and couldn't have more children."

Jeez. Ida Belle and I were twins separated by a mere forty-plus birth years.

I didn't say anything at all, afraid that if I opened my mouth, decades' worth of pent-up disappointment and anger would rush right out and flood us all. But Gertie's words gave me a new understanding of Ida Belle's refusal to marry the seemingly nice Walter, or any other man.

Ida Belle motioned for us to get moving. "You two going to stand there all day gossiping about my miserable childhood, or are we going to get out of this stench and into a hot shower?"

"I vote for hot shower," I said and jumped in the boat.

"What about the gator?" Gertie asked.

"I'll call someone to deal with it when we get back to Sinful," Ida Belle said.

"What's the big deal?" I asked. "It's not like a rotting corpse is going to change the bouquet of this place."

"Some people in Sinful have uses for it," Ida Belle said.

Recalling the stuffed-head shop on Main Street, I decided it was better not to know.

I took the shotgun from Gertie and helped her down into the boat, then pushed us back from the dock. Ida Belle fired up the engine and began the slow process of weaving across the lake and back to the bayou. Gertie's face was still flushed as she sat on the bench, and her hands shook as she laid the shotgun across her lap.

I studied Ida Belle through my mirrored sunglasses. The worry I expected to show on her face wasn't present. First, she looked reflective, then determined, but not even remotely stressed, anxious, or scared. Interesting. She wasn't in shock, yet the situation she'd just faced with the alligator would have sent most people's coping skills into overdrive.

Something about Ida Belle wasn't right. Despite the moonshine situation, I didn't think she was under the influence of anything that would have a calming effect, and so far, I hadn't seen any signs that she was a sociopath. But then if she was a smart one, I wouldn't see any signs.

As we left the lake and entered the winding bayou, I took in a deep breath of non-Number Two air and blew it slowly out. I was going to have to be more careful going forward. I'd taken Ida Belle and Gertie at their word on everything, despite warnings from Walter and Deputy LeBlanc not to get involved. Maybe there was more to the warning than I'd thought.

Maybe Ida Belle and Gertie had more to hide than moonshine.

———

IT TOOK TWO ROUNDS WITH SOAP, ONE WITH BODY SCRUB, and three shampoos before I was convinced the smell wasn't on me but instead impregnated my nasal cavity. As soon as I got out of the shower and got dressed, I was going straight downstairs and sticking my nose directly in a can of coffee grounds. If that didn't clear the bad smell out, it was hopeless.

I'd barely finished toweling dry when I heard banging at my front door. Ida Belle and Gertie had hightailed it after dropping me off, leaving so fast, the tires on Gertie's old Cadillac had screeched with the effort. They seemed as anxious to put some distance between us as I was, which was interesting. I knew my reason for taking a step back and assessing the situation, but I got the feeling they were taking a step back to avoid the assessment.

That only left Deputy LeBlanc.

The banging started again, and I could almost hear the aggravation with every echoing rap. He wouldn't have any knuckles left if he kept it up. I was going to take my time—leisurely pick out an outfit, even put on undergarments, and maybe even dry my glued-on hair before bothering to answer. Then the third round of banging began, this time on a window.

I wrapped the towel around me and stalked downstairs. If he broke a window, I might have to shoot him. And that would be a problem. Besides, all that noise on top of all the stench from this morning was starting to give me a headache.

I yanked open the front door and yelled, "What?"

A man I'd never seen before glared at me.

Late fifties. Spare tire around his waist and flab everywhere else. The only threat here was annoyance.

The man gave me a long up-and-down look, then shook his head. "I should have known not to expect any better from a piece-of-shit lawyer. Can't even bother to put on clothes to answer the door. Like we needed more trash in this town."

Lawyer? "And you are...?"

"Don't pretend like you don't know. I know those tricks you use, and I'm here to give you fair warning that I done hired my own attorney. I'm not letting that worthless bitch get away with this."

I took a couple of seconds to mull over the situation. Clearly, the man had been misinformed about who I was and what I was doing in Sinful, but at the moment, I knew of only one woman in need of an attorney. Further protesting my nonattorney status probably wouldn't get me anywhere, but if I goaded him, I might get something useful.

I smiled. "The worthless bitch and I look forward to meeting this attorney of yours, although I have no idea what you think you're going to accomplish."

"I'm gonna accomplish keeping that bitch from stealing any more money from my cousin's estate. God only knows how much she's blown through in the past five years, giving it away to charities and supporting that dummy brother of hers."

I nodded. "You're absolutely right. Giving to charity and taking care of one's family are horrible uses of one's own money."

A red flush started on his neck and crept up his face. "Don't get smart with me, girl. You know good and well she killed my cousin to get that money. It's taken five years, but it's all going to come out now. And there ain't a thing either of you can do about it."

"If that's the case, I don't guess I understand the purpose of your visit."

"I'm looking for Marie. I got papers to serve her. Legal documents that will prevent her from wasting any more of my cousin's money."

"You afraid there will be less left for you to take?"

"That money is rightfully mine! If Harvey would have known what kind of conniving trash he'd married, he would have written a will. In fact, we only have the word of the conniving trash that he didn't have a will."

"Well, until you can prove otherwise, I guess that word is the law."

"We'll see about that. So, where is she?"

"Who?"

"The conniving trash!"

I shrugged. "I don't know."

"I know you're hiding her somewhere. If I have to, I'll run you right over and search this house."

"No. You won't." The voice sounded from the side of the house.

I leaned out the front door to see Deputy LeBlanc making his way around the house into the front lawn. He didn't look happy.

The man gave Deputy LeBlanc a dirty look. "I know my rights. She can't hide Marie in there to avoid serving her papers." He looked back at me. "Maybe I'll just serve you instead."

"I wouldn't recommend that," I said.

"I don't give a shit what you recommend." He pulled a pack of papers from his shirt pocket and tossed them at me. "Consider you and your client served."

He whirled around and stomped off the porch and to his truck, a beat-up Chevy. The engine rolled several times and he banged his hand on the steering wheel. The engine caught, and he flew backward out of the driveway and screeched onto the street.

"Well, don't just stand there," I said.

Deputy LeBlanc stepped onto the porch and got his first clear look at me and my current wardrobe. His expression was a mixture of resignation and exhaustion.

"What would you like me to do?" he asked.

"Arrest him for assaulting my house."

"You're lucky I don't arrest you for being improperly dressed in public...again."

"He caught me in the shower. I was going to dress before I came down, but I lost it when he started banging on the window. So, I take it Harvey's cousin didn't inherit money like Harvey."

"All he inherited from his dad was a bunch of overdue bills and a house that was falling down and full of beer cans."

Interesting. "So he was unhappy that Marie got everything when Harvey disappeared?"

"'Unhappy' is putting it mildly."

"I guess Harvey was handing out money to him before he disappeared."

Deputy LeBlanc shook his head. "Not that I'm aware of. Harvey was the cheapest man in the world except when it came to himself."

"Then why aren't you investigating *that* guy for Harvey's murder? Sounds like a prime candidate to me."

"Who says I'm not? It's not your business either way."

I reached over to pick up the papers that were lying on the front porch. It was an order to appear in court the day after tomorrow, so the court could rule on the merit of freezing all Marie's assets. I glanced at the complainant. *Melvin Blanchard.*

"You shouldn't have those," Deputy LeBlanc said.

"I told him it wasn't a good idea to give them to me. Can I help it if he's an idiot?" I handed the papers to Deputy LeBlanc. "You know this means she doesn't have to appear. She hasn't been served."

"As soon as you find some clothes, you can report that to Ida Belle and Gertie and make them happy." He narrowed his green eyes at me. "You know you're asking for a heap of trouble, letting those two talk you into whatever they're up to. The only thing that can help Marie is a good defense attorney. She's not furthering her case by hiding."

"I know."

He sighed. "If you know that, then why are you helping them hide her?"

"I'm not."

"Sure you're not."

I felt my pulse spike and a flush creep up my neck. I wasn't opposed to lying, even on Sundays, but when I told the truth, I expected people to believe me. "Look—I just spent my morning slogging around on an island that smelled like a big turd, and Gertie was almost killed by an alligator. My nasal passages may never recover, and the worst part is, we didn't find Marie there. No one knows where she is."

He studied me for several seconds, and I saw something click in his expression. Finally, he believed me. He shook his head and sighed. "Did Ida Belle shoot the gator?"

"Yes. Don't tell me you're going to arrest her for that?"

"No, but at least I won't have to question Francine over where she got fresh alligator meat."

"You eat those things? Seriously?"

Deputy LeBlanc ignored my question and pointed a finger at me. "For a librarian, you seem to be in the middle of all the trouble happening in this town. Now, I've already told you once to back away. I suggest you listen when I tell you *this* time."

He whirled around and strode around the side of the house. I hurried into the kitchen and peeked out the blinds in time to see him head toward an aluminum boat that was pulled up onto the back lawn. He paused at the edge of the bayou and looked back at the house. I eased the blind down to a narrow slit.

He pushed the boat off the bank and jumped inside with admirable agility and balance. As he coasted away, he lifted his hand to wave.

I looked over at Bones, who'd opened one eye when I walked into the kitchen. "Some guard dog you are."

He yawned and closed the eye.

I stepped back from the window and blew out a breath. Deputy LeBlanc was beyond annoying. Even more so at the moment because he was right. I was in the middle of something that could get me splashed across newspapers, or even worse, television. Despite my makeup and hair extensions, there was a chance someone in Ahmad's organization would see the story and recognize me. At worst, I'd be killed. At best, Morrow would fire me. Neither sounded like good options.

But what concerned me even more was why the good deputy had been docked in my backyard to begin with. The hedges prevented a clear view of the driveway from the bayou, so he couldn't have seen Melvin's truck parked there. And the guy was loud, but I doubted seriously that he was loud enough to be heard through a house, across a fairly big lawn, and over a boat motor.

All of which meant that Deputy LeBlanc hadn't been cruising down the bayou and stopped off to prevent a fight. He'd obviously docked at the house for a completely different reason, and that made me really uncomfortable.

The back yard didn't hold any clues. The body hadn't been buried there; it had drifted along in the current until Bones dug it up. Marge was dead and gone, so hardly available to be pumped for information about Marie.

The only thing left that could be drawing him to the house was me. He knew I couldn't be involved in the murder, but he had every reason to suspect I was involved in a cover-up. I thought he'd believed me earlier when I told him about the trip to Number Two, and I was sure he'd get it all verified with Walter. But he still knew I was involved with whatever Gertie and Ida Belle were up to and likely figured I was going to stay that way.

Unless he can pressure you into leaving town.

It wasn't a pleasant thought, but a smart man might take that tactic. And despite my general dislike for Deputy LeBlanc, I didn't think for a moment that he was stupid. I might not be prone to the inner workings of small-town Louisiana, but I knew the three best ways to get someone to leave: kill them, threaten to kill them, or threaten to expose something they don't want exposed.

I wasn't worried about the first two, and if Deputy LeBlanc

got it in his head to run my prints, looking to find some dirt on me, he'd come up empty-handed. Morrow had seen to that himself. There was no trace of me left in federal databases.

But all it would take is a couple of phone calls to the right people and he might find out that the real Sandy-Sue Morrow was jet-setting in Europe. And that discovery would bring down the whole house of cards.

CHAPTER TEN

I FIXED A HAM SANDWICH, WENT INTO THE LIVING ROOM, and tried to concentrate on a hunting show on television. None of the so-called professionals on the show had a thing on Ida Belle, which was both impressive and worrisome at the same time. I was a trained assassin and wasn't sure I could have made the shot Ida Belle did under the same circumstances. At close range, I was excellent at hand-to-hand, or shoe-to-hand, combat, but I preferred to do my shooting from a distance and with a scope.

I swallowed the last bite of my sandwich and crumpled the napkin onto the plate sitting on the side table next to me. Who was I trying to fool—sitting here, pretending I wasn't spending every moment thinking about Marie, Melvin, Deputy LeBlanc, Ida Belle and Gertie, and the dark cloud of gloom that had descended on me ever since I'd arrived in Sinful? I could watch stupid television from now until the end of time, but the problem wasn't going away—not until someone found Marie and everything moved into the legal system.

Which left me right in Deputy LeBlanc's line of sight until

the case ceased being his responsibility and became the state prosecutor's problem.

I drummed my fingers on the table until the noise made me crazy. Finally, I grabbed the bag of cookies I'd been about to dive into, jumped up from the chair, and hurried out the door. I'd looked up Ida Belle's and Gertie's addresses on the Internet the other night when I was doing my research, but their telephone numbers had been unlisted.

I'd try Gertie's house first, and if they weren't there, I'd head to Ida Belle's next. It seemed the only way to ensure maintaining my cover was to find someone who didn't want to be found. It wasn't that much different from my real job, except the part about not having to kill anyone at the end of the mission. As the intended target was some kindly old lady who'd been abused by her husband and mother, I figured I could restrain myself.

Gertie's house was two blocks over from mine, so I stuck a cookie in my mouth and started out up the street, then made the turn around the corner to head to Gertie's. No sooner had I rounded the huge hedge on the corner than I ran straight into Deputy LeBlanc, who was parked next to the curb, securing his boat to the trailer.

Despite my quick pace and complete lack of braking, he didn't even budge when I slammed into his back. As he whirled around, I took a step back, a bit surprised at how solid he was. It seemed I had originally underestimated Deputy LeBlanc on almost every level.

"Sorry," I said, figuring taking the polite route would be best.

"In a hurry?"

"Just getting some exercise."

He looked down at the bag of chocolate chip cookies I had clutched in my hand, then raised one eyebrow.

"The cookies are the reason I have to exercise," I lied. "I'm not allowed to eat any unless I exercise while doing it."

He gave me a placating smile. "Sounds complicated."

"It works for me." I popped another cookie in my mouth. "Guess that means I have to run."

He put his hand on my arm before I took the first step. "I couldn't help but notice that your cookies were taking you the direction of Gertie's house."

"And? This entire town is the size of a postage stamp and is surrounded by bayous. Unless I plan on swimming, I'm going to be walking toward everyone's house, eventually."

"Hmmm. I thought maybe you were about to ignore my good advice about staying out of my murder investigation."

"I was not."

He stared at me, clearly not believing a word.

"I don't even know where she lives."

He studied my face, but he didn't have a chance. Lying was a huge part of my job. I'd been trained by the best forensic psychologists in the world. My own father wouldn't have been able to catch me lying by body language or facial expression.

Finally, he dropped his hand and gave me a single nod. "Try not to eat too many more of those. Trouble seems to follow you around. The thought of you roaming the streets makes me nervous."

"Ha. You've got man-eating monsters pretending to be frogs in your backyard, banana pudding wars, missing people, and an unsolved murder. I am the least of your worries."

Before he could get in another word or I could even see his expression, I stepped to his side and started off up the street at a good clip. Maybe he'd think about that and decide that checking into my background was a waste of time. As I approached Gertie's street, I slowed just a bit and made a show of looking up and down the street for traffic. I could still feel his eyes on me, but I wanted to verify that I hadn't lost my touch. I hadn't.

Damn.

I crossed the street and went into a park, the opposite direction of Gertie's house. I'd walk across the park to the bayou and circle around through the tree line to the row of houses behind Gertie's. Then I'd cut through to her house. I heard Deputy LeBlanc's truck engine fire up and the enormous tires turning on the pavement. A little girl and her mother were playing in a sandbox, so I stopped to pet her puppy, a roly-poly, happy, brown little thing. I heard the truck slow as it passed the park, but finally, it sped up and the noise of the obnoxious tires faded into the distance.

I said good-bye to the puppy and its people and continued on my original course to the bayou. The truck was gone, but Deputy LeBlanc could easily have rounded a corner and parked to spy on me. It was best I stick to my stealth plan. As I skirted the edge of the park around the bayou, I started to realize exactly how vast the swamp wasteland that surrounded Sinful really was. Narrow passages of water, which Ida Belle had called channels, stretched in every direction like wavy spiderwebs weaving across the land. If a piece of Harvey hadn't surfaced the day I arrived in town, I would have believed this the perfect place to dump a body.

Apparently, Marie had felt the same way.

The tree line curved to the left, and I trudged alongside it until I was behind the last row of houses that made up the town of Sinful. All I needed to do was find a way through that last row and into the block before it, and I'd be safely tucked away at Gertie's house. I scanned the backyards, looking for an entry point, but a row of eight-foot fences stared back at me. At the far end of the row of houses, the bayou curved around, cutting off access unless I wanted to swim. Circling back the other way put me right back in the open and exposed to Deputy LeBlanc, who might be lurking behind a bush.

Mind made up, I approached the row of fences. It was only eight feet. If I couldn't scale eight feet, I needed to go ahead and retire. Gertie's house was in the middle of the block, directly across the street from the row of houses I was behind, so I chose a stretch of fence in the middle.

I looked down at the bag of cookies and sighed before tossing the whole thing into the bayou. Then, I leapt up, grabbed the top row of the fence, and pulled myself up to peer into the yard. The last thing I needed was to run into a loud or angry dog.

The backyard was clear except for a barbecue pit, a single lawn chair, and a doghouse. A careful study of the doghouse proved it to be empty, so I pulled myself over the fence and jumped over the hedge that lined the back wall of the fence. I did a quick drop and roll, then bounced back up, ready to take off across the lawn. That's when I heard the rattle of a doorknob. I sprang back into the bushes, hoping my stay would be a temporary one.

An enormous Rottweiler bounded out the back door and hurried to the center of the lawn, where he stood scanning his domain, no doubt to ensure it was free of intruders. Before I could launch into panic mode, my training took over and I immediately modified my breathing to control my heartbeat.

Just wait it out.

With any luck, the owner had let him out to do his business, and he'd do it and go back inside. He sniffed the ground and then lifted his head and sniffed the air. I was certain he couldn't hear me as I hadn't moved a muscle and was barely breathing, but I knew he could smell me, or at least smell the apple-scented shampoo that the beauty shop had insisted I use on my fake hair. Finally, he turned and trotted over to a section of the fence on the side of the yard and hiked a leg. Slowly, I let out the breath I'd been holding.

He finished his business, then trotted back to the back door and barked. I felt relief wash over me. The owner would let him back in the house, and this would be just another minor delay in my trip to Gertie's. But when the back door opened, the dog did not walk in. Instead, the owner walked out.

Deputy LeBlanc!

I felt the blood rush out of my face. Of all the bushes in Sinful to hide in, I had managed to choose bushes that belonged to the one person I was trying desperately to avoid. No way would he take trespassing into his fenced backyard as part of my workout routine.

Using a single finger, I moved leaves out of the way to get a better view. Maybe he'd just stepped out to smoke or some-thing and would be heading back inside, complete with Rambo dog. My hopes were dashed when he set a plate of hamburger patties next to the grill, then opened the grill and lit the flame. Once the grill was lit, he sat in the lawn chair and lifted the beer he was holding in his other hand to take a drink.

This was *so* not good.

My chance of remaining undiscovered by the dog during the time it took for him to cook the stack of hamburger patties was so miniscule that it wasn't even worth calculating. The dog, standing next to the lawn chair so that Deputy LeBlanc could stroke his massive head, suddenly stiffened and looked straight at my hiding place. If I could have mentally willed myself to become a leaf, I would have done so.

After what seemed like an excruciating amount of time, the dog finally relaxed and sank to the ground next to the chair. At that moment, I felt a vibration in my pocket and struggled not to make a sound.

The cell phone.

Harrison had bought me a disposable cell phone before I left D.C. He was the only one with the number, and he wasn't supposed to use it unless there was an emergency. I felt my pulse increase as I abandoned my sniper breathing and eased the phone from my pocket, saying a prayer of thanks that the ringer hadn't been on.

I glanced at the display and saw I had a text message—from Gertie!

I didn't know or even care how she'd gotten my number. All I knew was that she'd just thrown me a lifeline. I watched Deputy LeBlanc consume his beer for a couple of minutes, then finally got the movement I'd been waiting on. He rose from the lawn chair to put the burgers on the grill. Immediately, I went to text messages, hoping the noise he made putting the burgers to cook would mask the sound of my texting.

Where are you? Need to talk.

That was the message from Gertie. No shit, we needed to talk. I kept one eye on the dog and used both hands to tap out my message, glad I'd bothered to develop texting-without-looking skills. I glanced down at my message to check it before sending.

Call Deputy LeBlanc at his home. I'll explain later.

I pressed Send, slipped the phone back in my pocket, and prayed. A couple of seconds later, I heard a phone ringing inside Deputy LeBlanc's house. He looked at the back door and frowned, and for a moment, I was afraid he was going to ignore it. Finally, he sighed, closed the cover on the grill, and walked inside. Unfortunately, he left Rambo Rottweiler outside.

As I hadn't given Gertie criteria for keeping him on the phone, I didn't have much time. Between the time constraint and the dog, crossing the backyard was completely out of the question. I picked up a rock from the landscaping bed and threw it at the fence in the far corner of the yard.

Rambo dog launched in that direction, and I spun and jumped for the top of the fence. I was halfway over before I realized a lock of my fake hair was caught in the bush. My head yanked backward and my eyes watered, but it was too late to stop the momentum. I tumbled over the top of the fence and the hair ripped from my head with a sickening tear.

I bit my bottom lip and held in a string of cursing as I ran for the tree line. I could hear Rambo dog barking at the fence behind me and the back door of Deputy LeBlanc's house bang shut as I dove into some brush at the edge of the swamp. I heard Deputy LeBlanc yell at the dog, and I froze behind the brush. If he found that piece of hair, I was sunk. Being Creole country, this wasn't exactly a town of women with long blond hair. Most of the hair I'd seen so far had been silver or gray.

I waited a couple of seconds more, then hurried through the brush and back into the park. As I burst out of the tree line into the playground, everyone stopped what they were doing and stared.

"Bird watching," I said, and hurried past.

I had one hand over the top of my head where the extension had torn out, and I could feel blood oozing between my fingers. I hurried away from the park before anyone called the sheriff to report a deranged-looking woman bleeding in a public park.

Now that I knew Deputy LeBlanc lived right across the street from Gertie, walking up the block and entering her house by the front door was clearly out. As much as I wanted to avoid scaling another fence, it looked inevitable. I passed Gertie's street and entered the neighborhood one street over. I was relieved to see that several of the homes didn't have fences that met on the sides. I would avoid at least one incident of fence jumping.

I picked the one closest to Gertie's house and hurried down the fence line, darting from one shrub to another in an effort to remain mostly out of sight. When I got to the back of Gertie's fence, I glanced around to make sure no one was looking, then hopped across her lawn. The back door was open, so I let myself inside her kitchen. I could hear Gertie talking at the front of the house, so I eased down the hall to peek around the corner.

She stood in the living room, peeking between the blinds on her front window. "You sound frustrated, Carter," she said. "You need to work on that attitude if you ever expect to be elected sheriff when Robert E. Lee retires."

I shook my head in admiration. She still had Deputy LeBlanc on the phone. Gertie had serious skills.

As I stepped into the living room, the hardwood floor creaked and Gertie spun around. Her relief was apparent as she broke out into a smile.

"Oh my goodness. I'm so sorry, Carter," she said. "I've just found my glasses in the refrigerator. I guess no one stole them after all."

She ended the call and dropped her cell phone on the couch before rushing over to me. "Are you injured? How badly?"

"I had a hair accident," I said. "I haven't had time to check it out."

"Come into the kitchen and I'll fix you up. I texted Ida Belle while I had Carter on the phone. She should be here any minute."

I followed Gertie back into the kitchen and sat in a chair at the end of the breakfast table. Gertie turned on the water in the sink and grabbed a clean dish towel from the drawer.

"I'll let this water warm up a little," she said. "It will be easier to lift the blood off your hair so I can see what kind of damage you did."

I still had my hand pressed on my head, but I couldn't feel blood rushing out any longer. Apparently, the worst was past. Gertie dampened the towel with warm water and was just starting to lift the blood from my scalp when Ida Belle burst through the back door, huffing like a freight train.

"Damn battery is dead on my car. I ran all the way over here from my house."

Gertie shook her head. "You live a block away."

"So, what's your point?"

"You really need to start exercising."

"I'm seventy-two. How many reasons before I die do you think I'll need to run?"

I piped up, "Banana pudding, man-eating alligators, texts from Gertie—"

"Fine. What the hell happened to your head?" Ida Belle narrowed her eyes at Gertie. "Did you shoot her?"

I stared at Ida Belle. "Is that a real problem around here?"

Gertie glared. "That thing with the mailman was an accident."

"Uh-huh. And what about the thing with the dishwasher repairman?"

Gertie grumbled and went back to dabbing at my scalp. "You have a couple of mishaps and everyone's labeling you."

A second later, a hunk of my fake hair fell off in her hand and Gertie shrieked, tossing the hair in the air.

For a woman who was already winded, and clearly out of shape, Ida Belle sprang from her chair like a criminal who'd just spotted the police. The blond and somewhat red extension landed in the middle of the table, and Ida Belle leaned forward to see what it was.

"Is that your hair?" She looked over at Gertie, her eyes wide. "You scalped her."

"She didn't scalp me," I said. Best to contain this before it got out of hand. "I scalped myself before I got here."

Gertie leaned over to inspect my head. "Well, for someone who just lost a wad of hair, you're certainly not bleeding much. There is only a little tear here."

"That's because it's not my real hair. It's extensions. They were glued to my real hair. I don't think much of the real stuff came out."

Ida Belle slipped back into her chair and stared at me, cocking her head to the side. "Why would a former beauty queen have hair so short she needed to glue some in?"

Crap! I had to come up with something plausible fast, or the two nosy Nellies would be suspicious. My mind raced, and then I remembered some woman who'd come into the beauty shop in tears when I was getting the extensions put in.

"There was a horrible accident with hair bleach," I said. "We had to shave it all off."

Their eyes widened and Gertie's mouth formed an O.

Ida Belle nodded. "Tilly Monroe did something similar a couple of years ago. Thought she was going to go from red to blond, but her hair turned green. So she tried to fix it and burnt it all up to her scalp. Had to wear a wig for a year. They only do that fancy glued hair stuff in New Orleans."

Gertie picked up the extension from the table and held it next to my head. "It doesn't look like this covers the entire bald spot."

"No, I lost a piece before this one. That's why it started bleeding in the first place."

Ida Belle leaned forward in her chair. "Lost it where?"

"In Deputy LeBlanc's bushes."

CHAPTER ELEVEN

GERTIE AND IDA BELLE BOTH EXPLODED AT ONCE.

"What were you doing in his lawn?"

"He's going to know we're up to something!"

I held up a hand to stop the outrage. "I didn't intend to be in his lawn. It was an accident." Then I explained my attempt to sneak to Gertie's house, my worry about Deputy LeBlanc watching me, my bright idea about cutting through a lawn, and the comedy of errors that followed.

When I was done, Ida Belle and Gertie looked at each other, their expressions unreadable; then they both started giggling, then laughing. Finally, Gertie sank into the chair next to me with a snort, unable to remain standing, she was laughing so hard.

I drummed my fingers on the table and waited for the hilarity to end. Finally, they took a few deep gasping breaths, Ida Belle wiped the tears from her eyes with the bottom of her blouse, and they sat back in their chairs.

"My word," Ida Belle said, "you have got to have the absolute worst luck in the world. The irony of your mother calling you Fortune is priceless."

Gertie nodded. "Maybe we should revert to your beauty days and call you Miss Fortune. Get it—misfortune?"

She started howling with laughter all over again. Ida Belle scrunched up her face, clearly trying to hold it in, but finally, a burst of air came barreling out and she started laughing again. I yanked the dish towel from Gertie's hand and began patting my sore head.

"Go ahead and keep laughing," I said. "You two will die long before me. I'll get plenty of peace and quiet then."

They sobered a bit and reduced their laughter to gasping for air.

"You have to admit," Gertie wheezed, "it is an odd coincidence. What are the odds that the one lawn you pick belonged to Carter?"

"One in forty, given the size of the neighborhood," I said, not nearly as convinced of the hilarity as they were. "It's not like I ran across him in Manhattan or something."

"And he caught you tossing your shoes into the bayou, trying to kill an alligator you thought was a frog, eating Sunday lunch with the Sinful Ladies, and the bone was found in your yard," Ida Belle pointed out. "That's a statistical improbability even for a town this size, especially given the amount of time you've been here."

I threw up my hands. "So, what am I supposed to do? You guys got me in the middle of this mess, and now it seems no matter what I do, the spotlight is on me."

"I am worried about that piece of hair you left behind," Gertie said. "If Carter finds it, he'll know for sure it's yours. Not many platinum blondes around here, and with me keeping him on the phone with all that unnecessary nonsense about my glasses, he probably already suspects something."

"We have to get that hair back," I said.

Ida Belle nodded. "You're right about that. Can't leave that hair in his bushes. Eventually, he'll get around to working on his lawn. Carter always works in his lawn when he's thinking hard on something."

My mind flashed back to the burgers and the beer. "Please don't tell me it's his day off."

Gertie bit her lower lip and looked at Ida Belle.

"I'm afraid so," Ida Belle said, "and as he won't have another for ten days, he'll probably tackle the lawn this afternoon."

"We've got to get him out of the house," I said.

"I don't know," Gertie said. "Carter is pretty strict about his days off. He doesn't get many."

"Even if there was a call, the sheriff would take it today," Ida Belle added.

"There has to be a way to get him out of his house," I said.

Ida Belle stared at the wall for a moment, then nodded. "There is one way." She looked at Gertie. "You still got those pictures that we took on your phone last week?"

Gertie smiled. "You're a genius!" She ran out of the room and returned seconds later with her cell phone. She passed it to Ida Belle, who pushed around on the display for a bit, then smiled.

"Now we wait," Ida Belle said.

"Wait for what?"

"It won't take long," Ida Belle said. "We'll watch from the living room window. As soon as he leaves, Fortune and I will go retrieve the hair. I'll be lookout at Carter's fence, and Gertie can pretend to water her front flower beds and watch the street."

Ida Belle hurried into the living room, Gertie right on her heels. In case they were right, I trailed behind. I'd just stepped up beside Gertie to peer out a crack in the blinds when Deputy LeBlanc's front door flew open and he ran out of the house. He had on one tennis shoe and was attempting to pull on the other one while he ran. Finally, he gave up and tossed it in his truck before jumping in and backing out of his driveway, tires screeching.

He barely rounded the corner at the end of the street when Ida Belle yanked open the front door and ran out of the house.

"What are you waiting on?" Gertie asked, waving me outside. "Go! Go!"

I ran out the door and across the street with Ida Belle, who slipped behind the hedges lining the front stretch of Deputy LeBlanc's fence. For an instant, I wondered what had prompted such a rush from the good deputy, but decided I was probably better off not knowing. I eased in the hedge beside Ida Belle and pulled myself up the fence to peer over.

"Is the dog there?" Ida Belle asked.

"I don't see him."

"Well, hurry up, then. If Gertie sees him coming back, she'll text me, and then I'll whistle."

"Got it," I said and flipped over the top of the fence and into the backyard.

I froze for a couple of seconds and scanned every corner, looking for Rambo dog, but unless he was hiding in the bushes, he wasn't outside. I ran across the yard to the back fence line where I saw the long blond hair sticking out of the hedge, the platinum strands shining like aluminum in the sunlight. I grabbed the end of it and pulled, but it was caught on the bush.

At least that's what I thought.

I realized how badly I'd calculated when, on the second tug, Rambo dog stuck his head out of the shrub and growled, the other end of the extension clamped in his massive jaws. I dropped the extension as if it were a hot poker and hauled ass across the lawn. Rambo dog launched out of the bushes right behind me.

I was fast, but there was no way I could make it to the front fence line without his catching me, so I ran toward the patio and jumped on top of Rambo's doghouse. He launched his massive frame up the side of the house, and I said a silent prayer of thanks when he slid down the side and sat on the patio, growling.

Ida Belle must have heard the racket, because a couple of seconds later, her face, flushed with the effort of climbing, appeared over the front fence.

"That is not good," she said.

"Tell me something I don't already know."

"Where's a cat when you need one," Ida Belle grumbled. "I'll go find something to distract him."

She disappeared back over the hedge. I hoped her idea of a distraction didn't involve firearms. I couldn't exactly blame Rambo for defending his property. It was his job, although he was looking less and less scary with that blond tress hanging out of his mouth. I assessed my options for escape, but the doghouse, the grill, and the lawn chair were the only structures in the yard. And no way could I make it to the fence with Rambo's steely gaze on me.

Then I remembered the burgers.

I leaned over as far as I could, and my fingers barely brushed the handle of the grill. I put more weight on my back leg and leaned in a tiny bit more so that I could pull open the top on the grill. Sure enough, the hamburger patties sat there half done. In the deputy's rush, he'd remembered to turn off the grill, but hadn't taken the time to take the burgers inside.

I grabbed the patty closest to me, tore off a little piece, and tossed it to Rambo. His eyes remained rolled up and fastened on me even as he lowered his head to sniff the meat. Then he stuck his huge tongue out and licked the scrap right up from the patio, the extension hanging from his jaw the entire time.

I was going to have to use the bait and switch.

I squatted down on the doghouse and stretched out my hand, just far enough for Rambo to smell the meat. His ears perked up and he immediately inched closer. I was only going to get one chance to get this right, and I was going to have to make it a fast one. One slip and my hand would be right there next to that platinum piece of hair.

I steadied myself as much as I could and leaned forward, ready to make my move. I held out the entire patty, trying to entice Rambo close enough to grab the hair. He eyed me for a bit, still suspicious, but finally, the taste of the burger won out and he took that last step toward me.

When he lunged for the patty, I grabbed the extension and pulled, flinging the patty behind me. Rambo didn't even hesitate before following the patty. I launched off the doghouse and ran for the fence line, praying that he chewed before he swallowed. I didn't even pause to look behind me before I heaved myself on top of the fence. A huge crash sounded behind me, and I glanced back in time to see Rambo tackle the grill, spilling the rest of the hamburger patties onto the patio. I flipped over the fence and into the hedges, breaking some branches and crashing into a startled Ida Belle.

We both tumbled out of the bushes and onto the lawn, rolling in one giant ball of hands and feet. I wound up on top and sprang up immediately, worried that I'd killed Ida Belle. I smiled as she launched into a stream of cussing. At least she was still alive. I extended my hand and helped her up from the lawn, then glanced across the street.

Gertie stood in her front yard, holding her water hose in one hand and her cell phone to her ear with the other. The end of the hose had flipped over into the open window of her car, and I could see water running out from the bottom of the door. She was staring directly at us, jaw dropped, which I took to be shock from our fall, but then she dropped her cell phone and started waving frantically.

"We better run," I said.

Ida Belle stopped wiping off her pants and hurried after me

as I sprinted across the street. Gertie dropped the hose, which got lodged in the passenger's side mirror and remained hanging over the car door, grabbed her cell phone, and ran to the front door to hold it open. Ida Belle and I dashed inside, and Gertie pulled the door closed behind us. I peeked out the front window just in time to see Deputy LeBlanc rounding the corner.

"Gertie, the hose!" I yelled.

Gertie gave me a blank stare for a split second, then wailed, "Oh no!"

"Not now!" Ida Belle grabbed Gertie's arm as she moved toward the door.

Deputy LeBlanc pulled into his driveway, slammed his truck door, then hurried back inside.

"That was close," I said.

"He looks mad," Ida Belle said.

"He's going to be madder when he realizes the dog ate all his hamburger patties," I said.

"Is that how you distracted him?" Ida Belle nodded. "Good thinking."

"Crap," Gertie said and started pressing buttons on her cell phone.

"Something wrong?" I asked.

"I need to call Margaret and tell her not to bring her cat over."

———

WE COULD HEAR DEPUTY LEBLANC'S OUTRAGED CRIES ALL the way across the street and through the walls of Gertie's house. Gertie took the yelling as an opportunity to go outside and turn off the water hose and open her car door. A tidal wave of water gushed onto the pavement. Ida Belle rushed out with what had to be a gallon box of baking soda. She opened all the car doors and sprinkled the stuff everywhere. I made a mental note not to ride with Gertie for a good while, maybe ten years or more.

Gertie slogged back inside and to the kitchen, her now-wet shoes tracking water across her hardwood floor. Ida Belle trailed behind her, wiping up the water with a dish towel. I followed them into the kitchen and took a seat across from Ida Belle as Gertie put on a pot of coffee.

"I don't suppose you have any baked goods around here, do you?" I asked. "I tossed my bag of cookies before I went over Deputy LeBlanc's fence."

Gertie nodded. "I'd just finished a pound cake when you called. It will be great with coffee."

Ida Belle pointed at Gertie's feet. "You need to take off those wet sneakers and put them on the back steps to dry. The last thing we need is you catching a cold when we've got things to do."

Gertie pulled off her tennis shoes and tossed them on the back steps. "Fortune, you never told me what you were coming over here for," she said as she started pouring coffee. "Wouldn't it have been easier to call?"

"I suppose so, but I don't have your phone number. I don't know how you got mine."

Gertie slid cups of coffee in front of me and Ida Belle, then sat down with her own cup. "Your phone was on the kitchen counter on Sunday. I got your number off it in case I needed it, and loaded mine and Ida Belle's into your contacts, which is empty, by the way."

"My old phone crapped out," I said, making an excuse. "I haven't had time to load names yet."

Gertie nodded. "Well, now that you know we're in the contacts, you don't have to take any more risks getting in touch with us."

"Which numbers did you give her?" Ida Belle asked.

Gertie looked offended. "The secret ones, of course."

"You have secret phones?" I asked.

"Absolutely," Ida Belle said. "We have phones registered in our names, but with Big Brother able to pull your records at a moment's notice, we decided to keep pay-as-you-go phones. We drive over to New Orleans once a month to pay cash for more minutes. That way, there's no trail."

"Do I even want to know why you two need untraceable phones?"

"Probably not," Ida Belle said.

As she was likely right, I didn't push the issue. "I was coming over to tell you about a run-in I had with Harvey's cousin." I went on to explain the door banging, ensuing conversation, ineffectual paper serving, and Deputy LeBlanc's observation of the exchange.

"Why didn't you guys tell me about him?" I asked. "We could have wasted a ton of time looking for another suspect and he was right in front of us. That guy has some serious anger issues."

Ida Belle shook her head. "The police checked into him first thing, but he's got an airtight alibi for when Harvey disappeared."

"Completely airtight?"

"He was doing a year in a New Orleans prison. He was in seven months before Harvey went missing and did another five months after. Unless Harvey was alive all that time and Melvin found him and killed him after he got out, there's no way he did it."

"Crap." Another great idea shot to hell.

I drummed my fingers on the table, and then another idea popped in my mind.

"Is it possible he could be working with a partner? Being in prison is the perfect alibi. Maybe he took advantage of that."

Ida Belle raised her eyebrows. "That's not a bad thought." She looked over at Gertie. "Who does Melvin hang out with?"

Gertie stared at Ida Belle for a couple of seconds, then slowly shook her head. "No one that I could imagine him trusting with something like murder. His friends and family should be on one of those stupid criminal shows."

"If they're anything like Melvin," I said, "I totally get that. But maybe he hooked up with someone different—someone outside of his family and usual buddies. If he thought he was getting Harvey's money, he could have afforded to pay a lot."

"Well," Ida Belle said, "he doesn't exactly run in high-class circles, so it's entirely possible he found someone to partner with."

I nodded. "The most likely person would be someone he met in prison but who was paroled before he was."

Gertie and Ida Belle perked up, but suddenly my mind latched onto the flaw in my logic and I sighed.

"Never mind," I said.

"Why?" Gertie asked.

"If Melvin had someone murder Harvey, he would have wanted the body to be discovered while he was in prison. That way, it was far more likely Marie would be tried for it, and he could have made a run at Harvey's money a long time ago."

Ida Belle frowned. "Maybe they had a plan but something went wrong."

"Like what?"

"Maybe they didn't want the body found right away so that the time of death range would be wide enough that Marie couldn't alibi all the time."

"So you're thinking they would have hid the body?"

Ida Belle nodded.

"Where?"

"Somewhere in the swamp, I'd imagine," Ida Belle said,

"but if an alligator managed to get a hold of it...Well, that might be why it took five years for some of Harvey to appear."

I blew out a breath. "It's thin. I mean, really thin."

"Too thin to direct suspicion away from Marie?" Gertie asked.

I nodded. "We need more than supposition."

"Like what?"

"A possible partner, for starters."

Ida Belle pursed her lips. "I think your point about him making friends in prison is a good one. I hear that kind of thing on the news, so it's no secret it goes on."

"Yeah, but we'd have to know who he met in prison, and I have no idea how we'd get that information."

"Oh, that's the easy part," Gertie said.

"It is?"

"We'll have Myrtle look it up for us. They keep records of cellmates at least, right?"

"That's Marie's cousin, the woman who works for the sheriff's department, right? She could get in a lot of trouble if she gets caught by Deputy LeBlanc. What if she won't do it?"

"Oh, she'll do it," Ida Belle said.

Her tone made it sound like Myrtle didn't have much of a choice. I wondered for a moment if Ida Belle had something on the woman. I didn't wonder for a second if she'd use it. I already knew she would. Ida Belle was clearly the wrong person to mess with in Sinful.

She was the Godfather, except silver-haired, female, and southern.

CHAPTER TWELVE

DESPITE THE ENORMOUS HUNK OF POUND CAKE I'D EATEN AT Gertie's house—and not even counting the second serving—I felt my stomach rumble as I scaled Gertie's back fence and headed home. Apparently my earlier sandwich and all that cake weren't enough to cover the energy I'd expended running from Rambo.

I really didn't feel like another sandwich, and I certainly wasn't going to attempt cooking, not with the way my luck had been lately, so I hurried home and washed my hair. The bald spot was easy to see if I left the hair down, but I could cover it nicely if it was drawn back in a ponytail, which was my preferred hairstyle anyway, as long as I was required to be girly.

I guessed I'd have to see about getting it fixed at one of those "fancy shops in New Orleans" that Ida Belle had talked about before someone noticed and started to wonder. Which reminded me that I needed to check with Walter and see if he had an ETA on that battery for Marge's Jeep. I didn't necessarily need a vehicle to traverse all four blocks of Sinful, but I couldn't exactly walk to New Orleans.

When I had everything cleaned and looking public-presentable again, I grabbed a book on Revolutionary War weapons that I'd found in the bedroom and headed to Main Street for Francine's Café. There wasn't any banana pudding on Monday, but my mouth watered thinking about the chicken-fried steak I'd had on Sunday. I could definitely stand a repeat of that meal, and maybe some cobbler. Gertie said they had cobbler every day and all of it was good. It was going to have to be fabulous to top Gertie's pound cake, but in the name of science, I was willing to sacrifice my stomach for the comparison.

Francine's was empty except for two gray-haired men sitting in the corner. They looked up in interest when I walked in the door, then leaned in and started whispering. I figured they hadn't seen anyone under the age of thirty in a decade, so there was probably some speculation of species on their part.

Francine gave me a wave from the grill, then sauntered over with her order pad. "I guess neither my food nor hanging out with the Sinful Ladies got you killed."

"Not yet, but the jury's still out on the Sinful Ladies."

"Ha. You're a fast study. The Catholics will be gunning for you after that dash you made on Sunday."

I blinked. Hell, I hadn't even been thinking along those lines. Jeez, now in addition to everyone else, I had to watch my back for the Catholics. "It's hard to live a quiet life in this town, isn't it?"

Francine laughed. "Yeah, people who haven't ever spent time in small towns, especially southern ones, always have some idea that it's slow-paced and full of nice people smiling and waving. The second part is mostly true, but there's never any shortage of drama. I think maybe the lack of things to do has people creating things to disagree about."

"Maybe," I said, although I wasn't convinced. Murder

seemed a bit extreme a reaction to boredom, and yet they'd had one right smack in the middle of Geriatric Land.

"You want something to eat, hon?"

"Yes. I'll take chicken-fried steak, mashed potatoes with gravy, corn, and extra rolls."

Francine nodded as she jotted the order on her pad. "And to wash it down?"

"I don't suppose you have beer?"

"No. Sinful's a dry town."

"You're kidding me." But now that I thought about it, I hadn't seen any alcohol in the general store when I'd picked up sandwich fixings and the cookies. The Sinful Ladies' "cough medicine" sales were looking more and more necessary.

"I wish I was. A couple of beers or a glass of wine never hurt anybody, but darn if we can get the vote to pass. People are afraid a bar might open right here on Main Street. There's two bars nearby, mind you, but you have to drive a couple miles out of town to get to them."

"I see. I keep forgetting how religious this town is."

"Oh, it's not religion, though that's the excuse they give every time it comes up. It's the men that doesn't want a bar in Sinful. It would probably put the other two out of business, and then the men would all be stuck doing whatever it is they drive out of town to hide from their wives right here in the middle of town where everyone could see."

"No women go to the bars?"

"No reputable ones." She slipped her pad into her apron. "The closest I can get you is root beer."

"Make it a root beer float." Root beer was almost perfect when ice cream was in it.

"You got it. Food'll be ready in about ten minutes," she said as she walked back into the kitchen.

"I'm not in a hurry," I said and opened the book to where

I'd left off the night before. Amazing what horrible weaponry they had to use back then. I couldn't imagine doing my job without the tools I had now. The farmers that had won this country had some serious balls.

I was so engrossed in the book that I didn't even hear him come in.

"Ms. Morrow." Deputy LeBlanc's voice sounded right next to my chair, and I jumped.

"Jesus. Do you always sneak up on people like that?"

"That seems an odd question coming from you, but hold that thought." He looked over at Francine, who was coming our way with my food.

She set the plate in front of me and looked at Deputy LeBlanc. "You want something to eat?"

"I'll take the special."

She gave him a puzzled look. "I thought you always grilled on your day off."

He frowned. "Well, *someone* decided to send pictures to Junior Baker of his wife skinny-dipping with his cousin. Junior and his cousin got into a fight at the Swamp Bar, and I was halfway there before they called me to say all parties had left and the scuffle was over. In the meantime, Tiny ate my burgers, which I rushed off and left on the grill."

Tiny? Was he kidding?

Francine shook her head. "That woman is going to be the death of one of those men."

"You're probably right. I just can't decide which one would be the better loss. Oh, Francine, put my dinner on Ms. Morrow's tab."

Francine's eyes widened, but she didn't say a word before she hurried off to the kitchen.

"Why on earth would I buy your dinner?" I asked. "I hope you don't think I sent those naked pictures. I don't even know those people."

"I have my own ideas about who sent them, but I'll probably never be able to prove it."

"Then I don't know why you think I owe you anything."

He shoved his hand in his pocket and pulled out three strands of platinum blond hair. "I found these wedged in between my dog's teeth. Right there along with what was left of my dinner. The hedge you broke will probably survive, but the least you owe me is a meal. If you hadn't gotten him riled, he would never have gone after my burgers."

Holy shit! *You're a trained professional*, I told myself as I struggled to maintain a blank expression.

"I have no idea what you're talking about."

He gave me an amused smile. "Is that the best you can do?"

He leaned forward and lowered his voice. "You know, peeping in people's houses is against the law, but if you really want to catch a glimpse of me that badly, let me know. I'm always willing to accommodate a pretty woman."

He winked and laid the strands of hair across my book before sauntering off to the corner to talk to the old guys. I felt a flush of heat run up my neck and struggled to maintain control. The nerve of him, thinking I hid in his bushes to catch him in his undies or something. What an ego!

"Do you want a refill?" Francine's voice sounded beside me.

Crap, I was losing my touch. That was two people in a row who had sneaked up on me in a public place.

I looked up and saw her pointing at the empty mug. "Sure," I said. Maybe another root beer float would sweeten my temperament.

She returned a couple minutes later with the float, and I was still fuming.

"Has he always been that cocky?" I asked as she placed the float on the table.

Francine glanced nervously at Deputy LeBlanc and then nodded. "He was always sorta the best at everything: good grades, football star, best hunter...All the girls in Sinful chased after him something fierce. I sometimes think he went into the Marines just to get away from them."

"Figures," I muttered. "So, where's his harem now?"

"Well, quite a few didn't feel like waiting around, so they married others, some left town for bigger things, but there's still a few vying for his attention."

She cocked her head to the side and studied me for a minute. "'Course, I haven't seen him pay any woman mind until you."

"Oh, no! I have absolutely no interest in Deputy Charming. In fact, if there was such a thing as negative interest, that's what I have."

"Deputy Charming. I like that."

"I'm sorta into sarcasm."

Francine shrugged. "Well, you could do a lot worse. I realize you're only here for the summer, but a little summer fling never hurt anyone. Well, except Maureen Thompson, but she was sleeping with her sister's husband."

She turned and walked back to the kitchen, leaving me stewing in my root beer float. Things were worse than ever. Not only had I risked my life to get that hair extension, only to have Tiny—and what an absurd name that was - clinging to evidence; but now Deputy LeBlanc assumed I was in his back-yard because I had some amorous intentions concerning him. What a nightmare.

As soon as I finished dessert, I was going straight home, climbing into bed, and not leaving the house for the rest of the day, unless there was a fire. Today was out of control. I needed time to decompress and regroup.

I have no idea what compelled me to look over at Deputy LeBlanc, but it was as if I couldn't help myself. He was still sitting with the old-timers, but as I glanced over, he looked straight at me, then winked.

I sighed. Maybe I'd just make a quick stop by Gertie's for some of that cough syrup before heading home.

CHAPTER THIRTEEN

I WAS POURING A SHOT OF COUGH SYRUP WHEN THE HOUSE phone rang. I paused for a second, feeling strange about answering a dead woman's phone, but then I figured everyone knew she was dead and someone was still calling, which meant the call was probably for me. I glanced at my watch. Eight o'clock. I answered the phone, expecting Gertie or Ida Belle to be on the other line, but got a proper-sounding male voice instead.

"Miss Morrow?"

"Yes."

"I'm sorry to call so late. This is Albert Worley. I'm an attorney with Worley and Pickard."

The summons!

"I'm sorry, Mr. Worley, but I can't help you find Marie. I don't even know the woman."

There was dead silence for a moment and I wondered if he'd hung up. Then he cleared his throat.

"I'm afraid I'm confused, Miss Morrow. I'm your late aunt's attorney."

"Oh. Oh! I'm sorry, Mr. Worley. There's been some drama

since I've arrived at my aunt's house, and I thought you were calling for a different reason."

Mr. Worley cleared his throat. "I hope everything is all right..."

"Everything's fine. A bit of a misunderstanding is all. How can I help you, Mr. Worley? I'm afraid I haven't even begun to catalog my aunt's belongings."

"We're in no hurry for that. Your aunt did quite well with her stock market investments, and the estate can handle the cost of your stay for as long as is necessary to wrap everything up."

"Oh, well, I'm really hoping to get everything settled before summer is over."

"That's fine, Ms. Morrow. I just wanted to make you aware that there's no pressure on our end of things. I know you live in a big city, but things tend to move at a slower pace in small places."

"That's what they tell me." I hadn't actually experienced it, but I was still hoping.

"The reason for my call is that your aunt left a document to be given to you following her death."

"What kind of document?"

"I'm afraid I don't know. It was sealed when she delivered it to us for safekeeping. Our instructions were to deliver it to you after her passing. If you'd like to pick it up at our office in New Orleans, that is fine, or I can arrange to meet you at your aunt's house. I would send it courier, but I need to get your signature for the estate's files."

Crap. The last thing I needed to do was forge Sandy-Sue's signature on legal documents. Besides, whatever Marge had written in that document, she intended for her niece to read it, not me.

"I'm not sure what my schedule is this week, Mr. Worley. My aunt's Jeep is currently out of commission, but I'm hoping it will be fixed soon. I need to make a trip to New Orleans after that repair is complete. Can I call you and let you know when that's planned?"

"Of course. As I said before, there's no rush. I'll make arrangements for whenever you're in town. Thank you, Ms. Morrow, and have a good evening."

I hung up the phone and headed upstairs with my bottle of cough syrup and shot glass in tow. I'd already had one shot, but I figured two would be better, especially if I intended to go to bed this early. I wasn't exactly the early-to-bed type. As the first shot had almost burned off my vocal cords, I didn't even want to imagine what it was doing to my bloodstream. I planned on being in pajamas and in bed before I went for round two. I was going to get some sleep around here if it killed me.

———

I WAS HALFWAY UP THE STAIRS WHEN MY CELL PHONE RANG. I groaned, not even remotely in the mood for a midnight jaunt with the two walking senior queens of trouble. I pulled the phone from my pocket, and my heart began to race as I saw the call was from Harrison.

"What the hell is going on down there?" Harrison's voice boomed over the cell phone as soon as I answered.

I froze on the stairwell. "What do you mean?"

"I have alerts imbedded in any search of the national databases. One popped last night for your dead aunt."

"Oh!" Deputy LeBlanc was moving quicker than I'd thought he would.

"Why is someone looking into a woman who died of natural causes?"

I explained the situation with the bone, leaving out my

involvement with the Senior Citizen Mafia of Sinful, as I was afraid it would give him apoplexy.

"Jesus, Redding, you're a magnet for dead people. Please tell me you're not involved in this."

"How could I be? The guy was killed a long time ago. Not like I could have done it."

"Well, apparently a Deputy LeBlanc thinks Aunt Marge knew something about it. Why else would he investigate her?"

"She was good friends with the dead man's wife, and I understand from the locals that the dead man was an abusive but wealthy asshole. Maybe Deputy LeBlanc thinks one of her friends helped her out of the problem."

"You've been talking to locals about this? Stop! You cannot get involved in this mess. Stick to packing boxes and watering plants or whatever else they do down there."

"You don't want to know," I muttered.

"What?"

"Nothing. Trust me, I'm trying to stay out of everything, but it would be odder if I wasn't curious. I'm not asking questions, but if people start gossiping, I'm not going to ask them to stop."

There was silence for a couple of seconds; then I heard Harrison sigh. "I get it. Fine, then listen, but do not offer an opinion on anything."

"I promise to keep my opinions to myself." *And Ida Belle and Gertie.*

Which reminded me. "Uh, Harrison," I said, "there might be some more names that pop. The dead woman was in some sort of old ladies society that seems to run this town."

"Okay. If any seniors pop, I'll know it's just the deputy fishing."

"Is there any news on my situation?"

"I'm afraid not. Ahmad's gone underground. Our intel went black, and we haven't locked on since Friday."

"But the hit is still out?"

"Yeah. We've intercepted communication to two known Brazilian assassins. We know they entered the country, but we haven't been able to locate them yet."

"Okay," I said, afraid to say more because I knew my disappointment would sound clearly through my voice.

"Listen, Redding. I'm really sorry about all this. I know we don't always see eye to eye, but that's about the work, not personal. I want you to know I'm doing everything I can to get you out of there. So is Morrow."

"I know." And I did know. Harrison and I fought like angry ex-lovers, and Morrow sometimes seemed to channel my late father with his disapproval and ass-chewing, but I knew they both wanted this resolved as much as I did.

"Okay," Harrison said. "I don't want to keep this line open too long. I won't call again unless the situation has changed, but keep checking your email. I'll give you updates when I can get a secure connection."

"Thanks—Harrison?"

"Yeah?"

"I appreciate everything you're doing."

"I know," he repeated my words back to me.

I disconnected and trudged up the stairs. So far, Deputy LeBlanc's research hadn't extended to me. Granted, there was no logical reason for it to as Sandy-Sue hadn't been anywhere near Sinful when Harvey disappeared, but I wondered at what point curiosity would get the better of him and he did a background check just because.

There were so many things for me to consider that my head was beginning to hurt. I was going to change clothes, get into bed with my book, and have some more cough syrup. With any luck, I'd fall into a coma and that would solve all my problems.

––––––

I was just about to slip on the headphones when I heard a board creak overhead. Immediately, I dropped the headphones onto the bed and slipped out from under the covers. The night air was desperately muggy and still and couldn't possibly have contributed to the noise.

Someone was in the attic.

During my original sweep of the house, I'd discovered the staircase to the attic at the end of the hallway. I'd thought it was a closet at first, but instead, I had found the narrowest set of stairs known to man. Nothing of any size could possibly be stored there as it would never make it up the staircase.

I pulled on my socks to silence my approach, then crept down the hall to the staircase door. I held my breath as I eased the door open, relieved when it didn't squeak, then slid into the narrow space and tiptoed up the steps until I could peek into the attic.

There was a single window at the end of the attic, and light from the full moon streamed in through it, creating a glimmering path down the center of the space. I cased the entire area, trying to make out some movement in the shadows, but everything was still.

Not even a whisper of air passed through, and for an instant, I wondered if I'd been mistaken.

Then I heard it again at the far end of the attic.

I inched into the space, praying that the floorboards didn't creak as I stepped onto them. I paused a moment, but only the silence of the attic echoed back at me. Whatever it was had gone still, which meant that it probably knew I was there —had sensed me, smelled me, or seen me. The element of surprise was out, but I still had the element of a pistol on my side.

On high alert, I crept across the attic floor, falling back

into combat mode, relying on all of my senses to give me any advantage. The sides of the attic were stacked with boxes and small furniture. Some of it was covered with sheets, giving the entire place the appearance of one of those houses you saw in a horror movie.

And here I was, blond, in my pajamas, and creeping up on whatever was in there with me instead of getting out of the house. It would be a total cliché except that I wasn't well-endowed or a cheerleader and would have easily dispatched those wimps from *Scream*.

At the end of the attic, the stacks of boxes rose higher, almost touching the ceiling. What in the world was Marge storing up here? I had one closet in my tiny apartment back in D.C., and if you removed the weapons, it wouldn't be a quarter full of anything else.

I took a couple of steps toward the boxes and that's when I saw one of the sheets covering some of them move. The movement was at shoulder level, and I froze, instantly realizing that if those boxes did not extend to the side wall of the house, someone could easily be hiding behind them. Someone with a rifle trained in between those boxes and pointing at my head.

In a split second, I launched at the boxes and ripped the sheet from the top, then ducked before they could get off a shot at me. But my problem turned out to be of a completely different sort. As I ducked down, something large and furry landed right on my shoulder. All I could see was the flash of white from eyes and teeth.

I didn't scream. A trained assassin does not scream, even when attacked by fur with teeth, but I did put a round through the roof of the attic, trying to hit the thing. I was unsuccessful. The furry teeth scurried across the attic floor to the far end, ran up an old bookcase, opened the window and sprang into the tree outside.

I ran after it, thinking I might be able to pick it off in the tree, tripped over a coatrack and went sprawling into a stack of boxes, bringing them down on top of me. I scrambled out of the mess and ran to the window, but Furry Teeth was long gone. Disgusted, I closed the window, locked it this time, then swung around in a huff and banged my foot on a box. Aggravated, I kicked the offending box for good measure and the old cardboard split, heaving the contents onto the attic floor.

The glint of a military medal caught my eye and I stooped to see it was attached to a very old army uniform that I recognized as from the Vietnam era. I lifted the jacket up for a closer view and saw Marge's name stitched on it. So Marge was a Vietnam veteran, and from the looks of the stripes and medals, had not been over there painting her fingernails. This woman had seen some serious action.

A military career certainly explained the simplicity and organization of her home, not to mention that it shed a ton of light on her reading material. And maybe it somehow explained why I felt so comfortable in her home even though I was completely out of my element everywhere else.

Honor and respect wouldn't allow me to leave a stack of military triumph rumpled on the floor in the attic, so I scooped the uniforms back into the box and picked the whole thing up, encircling the broken side with my left arm. Tomorrow, I could press all the clothes and find a more suitable container for them.

I headed back downstairs to the bedroom and set the entire box of items on the desk. One glance at my watch had me groaning. Two a.m. Only five hours left to get some sleep before my internal alarm clock went off and I started another day of bliss in Sinful. Louisiana was hell on the sleeping population. I was starting to wonder if the people living here were vampires.

I reloaded the pistol and picked up the headphones, ready to make the most of the little bit of sleeping time I had left.

But before I got them on, someone started banging on my front door. What in the world was the problem now?

I stomped downstairs and flung open the door. Deputy LeBlanc stood on the front porch, looking rumpled, exhausted, and not any happier than I was.

"What now?" I asked.

"I got a call about shots fired in this area."

"And naturally, you assumed it was me."

"Naturally."

I started to deny it, but as I was going to have to hire someone to repair the roof, I figured it would get out anyway. "There was something in the attic. I fired some shots at it, but it got away."

He raised one eyebrow. "Got away how?"

"Darn thing opened the window and shimmied down the tree outside. I wasn't aware that monkeys were native to the swamp, but then I'll admit I don't know much about the state."

He sighed. "The only monkeys in this state are in a zoo or holding political office. If it opened the window, it was a raccoon. They have opposable thumbs and are very clever. They are also essentially harmless."

"The thing attacked me! Jumped on me, then ran me over."

"It didn't attack you. You startled it and it scrambled to get out of the attic when you tried to kill it. The real question is, where did you get the pistol?"

Uh-oh. "Walter sold me a rifle."

"And if that's what you had fired, I wouldn't have as big a problem. People here know the difference between a rifle and pistol shot. And as I personally removed all the weapons from Marge's house after her death, I know it wasn't readily available."

"You removed the weapons? That's my inheritance! What gave you the right to take it?"

"The guns are safe and sound and locked away at the sheriff's department, but I wasn't about to let an empty house sit around with loaded guns in it, especially when everyone in town knew they were here."

"Okay, but what's your excuse for keeping them now?"

"I was going to return them when you arrived, but once I met you, I had second thoughts...and thirds, and fourths. Turns out I was right as you've probably shot a hole in your own roof."

I tried to come up with a good argument, but had to admit, he sorta had me on this one, which didn't do anything at all to improve my mood.

"I'm going to assume," he continued, "that Walter, in his misguided attempts to take care of a pretty woman, loaned you his pistol. I expect you to return it to him tomorrow or both of you will be hearing from me."

He pulled out a pad of tickets and I felt my blood pressure rise.

"You're writing me a ticket? Let me guess—it's against the law to startle wild animals in your own house on Tuesdays?"

He ignored me completely and kept writing, then tore the paper off the pad and handed it to me. I looked down at it, but all it had was the name "Buddy" and a phone number.

"Buddy will fix the roof," he said. "Make sure he's sober when he starts or he'll fall off and his wife will have to put up with him underfoot for the six weeks it takes that bum leg of his to heal. I've known Buddy my whole life, and trust me, no one deserves that aggravation."

"Sober. Got it. And thanks."

He nodded. "Now, please put on your headphones and go to sleep before something ends up injured or worse. At least unload that pistol until I get some backup that's not half blind and hard of hearing. I haven't gotten a good night's sleep since you showed up."

He stepped off the porch and crossed the lawn to his truck.

"That makes two of us," I yelled as he pulled away from the curb.

I looked across the street and saw curtains drop back into place. Bunch of nosy people in this town. I slammed the front door, just because I could, and heard something in the bedroom above me hit the floor with a thud. I hurried back up the stairs to find the box from the attic dumped over on the floor. I must have left it too close to the edge of the desk, and the vibration from my slamming the door like a degenerate had caused it to fall over.

Bones, who hadn't awakened for the noise upstairs, the killing of the roof, or Deputy LeBlanc's visit, chose that moment to start howling. I walked out of the bedroom and looked down the stairwell to see him trying to come up the stairs. He wasn't even remotely successful, and the second time he slipped, I decided I'd better go downstairs and restrain him before I had another death on my hands.

It took two treats and the twenty minutes Bones gummed them to get the dog calmed down and back to sleep. I trudged upstairs again, thinking that I got more rest and had less drama when I was on an assassin job. I stopped short and sighed when I saw the contents of the box still scattered across the bedroom floor.

Completely over the worn-out box, the raccoon, the "borrowed" pistol, and the entire loss of another night, I started stacking the uniforms in some semblance of order on the desk. When I pulled the last one up from the floor, a set of bundled envelopes fell out and onto the floor. I picked them up, expecting to find letters from family and friends to Marge that were sent during the war, but was surprised to find the front of the envelopes blank.

I removed the heavy rubber band from the bundle and

opened the flap on one of the envelopes to slip out the paper inside.

SEPTEMBER 7, 1961

Things are dire here in the jungle, but I remain safe as long as I stay focused on the job I'm here to do. Despite the attention I give my work, I find myself thinking of you at the oddest times. Sometimes I think of the way we walk down Main Street every year for the Fall Festival. Or the look on your face when we got stuck on the top of the Ferris wheel at the county fair. I miss your smile when we take a boat ride and the way you laugh at old silly black and white movies.

I've always loved you. The distance between us and the sacrifices I make every day for the sake of freedom have not diminished that certainty. Would that I could but tell you my deepest feelings, and my heart would not be as heavy as it is now, carrying this secret alone.

Marge

I PULLED THE PAPER OUT OF THE NEXT ENVELOPE AND FOUND a similar letter. The thoughts and dreams of a soldier who missed her loved one. Flipping through the stack, I realized there had to be fifty envelopes, but not a single one was addressed.

Marge had written all those letters to the man she loved, but never mailed them.

I put the envelopes on the desk next to the uniforms, turned off the lamp, and crawled into bed. But as I lay in the dark, my mind whirled instead of relaxing into sleep. What must it feel like to love someone so completely? To be in the midst of a horrible war, but have your mind wandering to the smile of that person you left behind?

I'd never cared about anyone like that. I wasn't even sure that I could.

There had been men, but I wouldn't even call what I'd had with them relationships, much less undying love. I couldn't even wrap my mind around writing all these letters but never having the courage to mail them. What could possibly be lost in doing so? If someone didn't feel the same as you, then surely knowing that was better than never knowing. And if they *did* return your feelings, then you might have a future.

I blew out a breath and forced myself to shut my eyes and start counting hand grenades. I was already neck deep in things I was unqualified to handle and had no business being involved in. The last thing I needed to add to the mix was the mystery of a fifty-year-old unrequited love affair.

But even as I slipped off to sleep, I found myself wondering if Marge had ever told him her feelings and if his answer was why those letters had remained unaddressed and in her possession all these years.

CHAPTER FOURTEEN

THE GLOW OF DAYLIGHT PEEKED THROUGH THE CURTAINS OF my bedroom, and I opened one eye to look at the clock on the nightstand. Nine o'clock! Surely that wasn't right. I opened the other eye, but there it was, nine a.m. staring back at me in big white numbering.

I wasn't sure whether to be appreciative or worried.

On one hand, I'd finally gotten decent sleep. On the other hand, I'd expected Ida Belle and Gertie to be pounding on my door hours before now and wondered why they hadn't. How sad was that? I'd been in town all of three days and was already conditioned to having people wake me up at the crack of dawn.

I sat up and removed the headphones, then stretched. Bones would want his breakfast and a bathroom break, so I went downstairs to roust him from his bed.

I roused Bones, who wandered into the living room instead of outside and stood at the bottom of the stairs braying again.

"What is up with you?" I asked as I struggled to pull the hound out of the living room and back into the kitchen.

I finally managed to get him turned around and out the

back door, then opened the refrigerator. A whole lot of blank space glared back at me. After we'd returned from Number Two, I'd nabbed my headphones and the other miscellaneous supplies from Walter, but only lingered long enough to grab bread, lunch meat, and the cookies I'd lost yesterday. After my mad dash for the shower, I'd intended to go back and shop more extensively for staples, but the day had gotten away from me after that, and I'd never made it back.

As I had to return the pistol to Walter, a trip to the general store was in order, assuming I wanted to eat on a semi-regular basis without paying Francine. I could check on the car battery situation while I was there. I needed that Jeep running so I could make a trip to New Orleans, and I wasn't about to trust Gertie to take me, especially as she'd played Noah-and-the-flood with her car yesterday. Besides, Ida Belle had alerted me to the fact that Gertie needed glasses to drive but wouldn't wear them.

My stomach rumbled as I closed the refrigerator door. I remembered CIA Assistant Reynolds saying once that it wasn't a good idea to go shopping on an empty stomach, so I made the executive decision that breakfast at Francine's was a requirement for making good decisions later on.

I grabbed some money from my sock drawer, threw on jeans, a T-shirt, and tennis shoes, grabbed my book, and headed out in a slow jog for Francine's. I figured jogging the two blocks might make up for a tenth of what I was likely to eat.

There were only four other customers in the café—two older couples—but a long table in the corner looked as if it had seen a food fight just before I'd arrived. Crumbs of whatever that was littered every square inch of the checked cloth and the surrounding floor. Tipped glasses of milk appeared every couple of feet across the tabletop. Someone clearly needed better table manners.

I took a seat at the corner table where I'd sat the day before and vowed this time not to get so absorbed in my book that anyone could sneak up on me again. The door to the kitchen swung open and I expected Francine to walk out, but instead, a young girl with long brown hair and pretty green eyes walked toward me, an order pad in her hand.

Mid-twenties, five foot six, good muscle tone and flexibility.

Easily the third healthiest person I'd seen in Sinful behind me and Deputy LeBlanc. She stepped up to the table and smiled.

"You must be Marge's niece. I've heard about you."

"Whatever Deputy LeBlanc said about me is an exaggeration. Probably."

She laughed. "Wasn't him that was talking, but you've definitely piqued my interest now. Celia Arceneaux is my aunt. She had plenty to say about your banana pudding dash on Sunday."

I looked up at her, a bit dismayed. "You're not going to refuse to serve me, are you?"

"Lord, no! I don't mix myself up with anything that silly bunch of old women have going on, which aggrieves my aunt to no end. She thinks because I work here I should have some sort of pull with Francine."

"You don't?"

"Nobody has pull with Francine, not even her husband. The woman is as practical and hardheaded as the day is long. She takes not getting involved with the townspeople's drama to a whole new level."

"Probably smart of her," I grumbled, thinking how much easier the past three days would have been if I had stayed out of the local drama.

"Heavens, I've totally forgotten my manners," the young woman said. "My name is Ally." She extended her hand.

I shook her hand, my opinion of this direct, fresh woman favorable so far.

"I'm Sandy-Sue," I said, trying hard not to blanch, "but everyone calls me Fortune."

"I like that," she said.

"Thanks." I pointed to the messy table. "What happened over there—they didn't like the food?"

"It was the mommies." Ally rolled her eyes. "They all come in here with their toddlers after dropping the older kids off at school. I'm afraid to think what their houses look like."

"What time is that?" I asked, a bit horrified. "I want to make sure I'm never here then."

Ally laughed. "They usually show up around eight and are gone by nine. So anytime before or after and you're good. Fortunately, the café and the park are usually the only places they frequent, so it's easy to avoid the fray."

I made a mental note.

"Well," Ally said, "I guess I best get your order in. I go on break in a couple of minutes and Oscar, the cook, will fill in for a bit. He's not exactly a people person."

I don't know what possessed me—maybe it was because she was friendly and didn't seem to have an agenda. Maybe it was loneliness. Most likely it was because I figured I could pump her for information on the townspeople. Regardless of the reason, I found myself inviting her to eat breakfast with me.

She smiled again. "I'd love to. I had a bagel this morning before we got started, but I burned it off hours ago. Let me get your order, and I'll bring it all out when it's ready. Then we can have us a nice chat."

She handed me a laminated card with the breakfast items, and I laughed at the list: Sinful Special, Without Sin, Mortal Sin, The Seven Deadly Sins, Create Your Own Sin.

"The lunch menu doesn't look like this at all," I said.

"The lunch menu is different since we serve that one meal on Sunday. But as no breakfast is served on Sunday, we get to use the irreverent menu. Francine's got a wicked sense of humor."

"And really good taste in food. Give me the Seven Deadly Sins." Eggs, bacon, sausage, biscuits, gravy, pan-fried potatoes, and pancakes. I could practically hear my arteries hardening.

"You got it. Give me about five minutes."

I opened my book, figuring I could probably get in a couple of pages before the food was ready. I was several pages into the chapter on explosives when Ally returned with a tray of food fit for an army. She started shifting plates from the tray to the table, and my mouth watered as I took in all the southern goodness.

"Is it all going to fit on the table?" I asked.

"Oh, sure," Ally said. "We may look like we're at a buffet by the time I'm done, but it will fit."

When she eased the last plate onto the table, there was only a tiny hole left for the ketchup that she pulled out of her apron.

"You don't know what a treat it is," she said as she took a seat across from me, "to have a meal with another single woman under the age of sixty."

"Based on the last couple of days, I understand completely," I said and then stuffed a huge forkful of pan-fried potatoes into my mouth and closed my eyes while I savored the incredible combination of perfectly-cooked potato slices, seasoning, and onions.

I swallowed and let out a sigh before opening my eyes. Ally looked amused.

"Do I need to get you and the potatoes a private room?" she asked.

"No. I'll settle for public display of affection with the potatoes, but I may take you up on that offer when I get to the pancakes."

Ally laughed. "When I heard about you coming to Sinful, I didn't imagine you'd be so entertaining."

"Why not?" I asked, curious about what was said before my arrival.

"I guess I heard beauty queen and librarian and didn't put the two together as fun or someone I'd enjoy having breakfast with." She looked a bit sheepish. "I went to school with a beauty pageant girl. We didn't exactly get along."

"I think I saw her Facebook page," I replied. "I don't blame you for not getting along. It was insipid. And for the record, all the beauty pageant stuff was my mother's doing. I haven't had anything to do with that since I started paying my own bills."

"Fair enough."

"So, I noticed there doesn't seem to be an abundance of younger people around here," I said. "I guess the mommies are at the park or closed in houses with their little darlings, but where are their men?"

"There's not a lot of employment here, so a lot of the men work construction in New Orleans during the week, or on oil rigs. The construction guys are usually around on Saturdays at the general store. The oil workers usually do two weeks on, two off, and right now, they're gone. The women are tied up with kids and making ends meet, so you don't see them out much. It's an old-fashioned town when it comes to women and careers."

"And the single ones?"

"Not many single men worth speaking of. Girls tend to snap up the decent ones, and any girl that's not looking to settle down or didn't get paired up by high school leaves town for a bigger pool of fish."

I glanced at her bare hand. "So, what's your story? You're smart, and I bet you'd have no trouble snapping up a guy, whatever that means, but you're here, no children attached, and well below the average age group."

Ally sighed. "I almost got away. My dad died when I was a teen, Momma didn't have any job skills to speak of. She was a receptionist at a dispatch office the next town over. There was no money for college, so I worked at the café several years after high school to pay for my first two years. I figured I could get a part-time in New Orleans to pay for the rest while I was going to school. But then Momma got sick my junior year."

"And you came home to take care of her?"

Ally nodded. "Francine was a lifesaver and gave me my old job back, and I've been doing some online courses when they're available, but they don't offer a lot of courses online for a nursing degree."

"And your mother—how's she doing?"

"She's dying...Cancer. One of those painful kinds that can take you in months or stretch into years. Momma's going on three years now."

"Wow. I'm really sorry. That's got to be hard."

"Oh, it's been out of my hands for a month now. She finally got so bad that the doctors insisted she go to a nursing home in New Orleans."

"Then why are you still here?"

She shrugged. "I don't know. I mean, when I was going to school, I knew absolutely that I wanted to be a nurse and live in the city. Then I came back home to take care of Momma, and all of a sudden, it didn't look as good."

"Maybe it's just cold feet over getting back into school."

"Maybe," she said, but she didn't sound convinced. She lifted up a spoonful of oatmeal, then set it back down in the bowl and looked directly at me. "Did you ever think you had all the answers when you were in the thick of something, but then when you take a step back, you realize you were so busy getting things done that you never stopped to ask yourself if it's what you really want to do?"

Her words slammed into me like a freight train. Back in

D.C., I always kept busy. If I wasn't working, I was thinking about work, preparing for work, or reviewing past work to identify areas that needed improvement. I didn't allow myself to slow down, much less step back. Maybe because I was afraid I'd ask the same questions Ally was asking herself. And I knew I had no good answers.

I realized that I'd never answered, but I had no idea what to say. Finally, I decided the truth was as good as anything and didn't give anything away. "I guess I never thought about it. I've been on autopilot for a long time."

Ally nodded. "If Momma hadn't gotten sick, I would have stayed in New Orleans, finished school, and probably gotten a job there. I think sometimes it takes a life-changing event to make us really see the way we're living based on the choices we've made.

"I can see that."

"Maybe one day, you'll have an event and it will cause you to rethink everything."

Like having a price on my head and hiding out in the swamp, pretending to be an ex-beauty queen?

"Maybe you'll be lucky," Ally continued, "and you'll think your choices are the right ones."

"Somehow, I doubt it. That hindsight thing and all. I'd guess most people aren't happy with everything they've done."

Except my father. Mr. Perfection.

"That's true," Ally agreed.

"So, have you figured out what you want to do?"

"I think so, but you'll probably think I'm crazy."

"You are the least crazy person I've met since I arrived. The upside of that is that nothing you say could surprise me."

She grinned. "I want to own a bakery and make beautiful, fancy desserts."

"I assume you don't mean in Sinful."

"No. A bakery wouldn't work in Sinful. People don't have

the money for fancy desserts, and most of the women here can bake like nobody's business anyway. But a little shop in downtown New Orleans would be a dream. Fresh coffee brewing all day...people walking in from the street to buy chocolates and then returning for wedding cakes and party trays."

She sighed. "Like it could ever happen."

I shrugged. "Why not? You can go to culinary school and work for a bakery while you're finishing. That way, you learn all the cool stuff they don't teach you in classrooms or books."

"Yes, that's true enough. I guess the part I get stuck on is capital to open a business. I wouldn't make much in a bakery, and Lord knows, Momma's house will probably barely cover the medical bills."

"So stay here a bit and save up. It's got to be cheaper than New Orleans, especially as you've got a free place to stay. Save more once you're in school and working and then apply for one of those grants."

She stared at me for a moment, her brow wrinkled, and I could tell her mind was working through the details. Finally, she nodded. "You're right. I need to start working on a plan, instead of just sitting here and feeling sorry for myself."

"That's okay. Anytime you need to sit around, eating this kind of food, and feeling sorry for yourself, I'll be happy to sit with you and tell you to stop."

She laughed. "It's a deal."

"And if you want to start practicing your baking and need a tester, I'm up for that, too." I glanced down at her bowl of oatmeal, the only plate on the table that was hers. "That oatmeal seems a lonely choice for a prospective baker."

"Clearly, I don't have your metabolism. If I ate all this, I'd be in a coma. Do you have a workout routine?"

"Mostly running and stress." *Especially lately*.

"I don't want any more stress, but maybe I'll take up running if it keeps you that fit."

"You could always run from the police. That would cover the running part and the stress part." It certainly had for me the day before.

She laughed. "I had something a little less interesting in mind."

Don't we all? "So, tell me, what's the deal with the Sinful Ladies Society?"

Ally glanced at the couples in the corner and then leaned in toward me. "Momma always called them the Geritol Mafia. They've been running Sinful for as long as most people can remember."

"But running it how? I mean, they look like harmless, old ladies." I didn't buy that for a second, but I figured I'd get more information by playing dumb.

Ally frowned. "I know. I said the same thing to Momma once, but she shook her head and told me I should never underestimate a clever woman. She said anything Ida Belle wanted done in Sinful, she figured out a way to make it happen, but I never heard her raise her voice or even ask someone for a favor. I have no idea how she manages it all."

I remembered the photos Gertie had sent to that unsuspecting husband to get Deputy LeBlanc out of his house.

"Blackmail?" I suggested.

Ally shrugged. "I guess anything's possible. There's a whole lot more that goes on in small towns than what people imagine."

"Given that a human bone washed up in my backyard on my first day in town, I'm not about to argue with you."

"That's a bad deal. There's been a lot of talk that the bone was Harvey Chicoron's, although the sheriff hasn't said for sure."

"I hear Harvey wasn't very well liked."

"That's a gross understatement, really. Most people who'd known him for more than five minutes loathed him."

"Sounds like a good riddance, then."

Ally nodded, but she looked worried. "The problem is, people are saying his wife, Marie, did it. Everyone loves Marie, and no one would blame her for doing it, but we don't want to see her go to prison, either."

"What does Marie say?"

Ally's eyes widened. "I thought Gertie or Ida Belle would have told you—Marie's missing. Deputy LeBlanc is madder than a hornet although he's trying not to let on."

"That doesn't exactly help her case. So, where do people think she is?"

"No one knows, but I'm starting to hope it's someplace where there's no extradition."

I took a bite of pancakes and held in a sigh.

I was hoping the same thing.

CHAPTER FIFTEEN

I WAS SO STUFFED WHEN I LEFT FRANCINE'S THAT I DECIDED I needed to skip eating for a while, at least until supper. I'd enjoyed talking to Ally, which sorta surprised me as the only women I'd had any sort of personal conversation with more than once and for more than a couple of minutes were the D.C. coroner and Hadley. Talking to Ally had also given me an idea. Ally was young and had been away for a while, so she wouldn't know all the past sins and secrets of the town, but I'd bet money that Walter would.

He sat in the general store every day, chatting with customers and watching the ebb and flow of the locals. Not to mention that he kept proposing to the object of my curiosity. If Walter didn't know how Ida Belle got things done, I'd concede she had them all hypnotized. I also figured it would be interesting to get a man's take on Harvey and Marie. So far, the only male who had been involved on any level was Deputy LeBlanc, but he was keeping all his opinions to himself, except the ones he had about me.

Thoughts of Deputy LeBlanc made me briefly wonder what he'd make of it if he caught me talking to Walter, but he *had* told me to return the pistol. So, technically speaking, it would be his fault if I returned the pistol and it led to conversation. After all, it would be bad manners, especially in the South, to walk into a man's store, hand him a gun, and not even ask how his day was.

Mind made up, I returned home, roused Bones from his nap on the porch and back into the kitchen, grabbed the pistol and headed to the general store.

Walter was in his usual spot behind the counter, sitting on a stool and reading the newspaper. He looked over his paper when I walked in and shook his head. "I guess the headphones didn't work so well," he said.

I stepped up to the counter and pulled up a stool to sit, assuming he was referring to the unfortunate raccoon incident. "Deputy LeBlanc has been talking about me again, hasn't he? If he keeps it up, I'm going to assume he's flirting."

Walter grinned. "Well, now, that might just be the case. Carter usually tries to avoid women as a species, but he does seem to have you in his rifle sights."

"Speaking of which," I said as I pulled the pistol from my waistband and passed it back to Walter, "he told me I had to return this. I hope I didn't get you into any trouble."

Walter stuck the pistol under the counter and waved a hand in dismissal. "All Carter did was give me a disapproving look. He knows better than to do more. After his dad died, I darn near raised the boy. He's my nephew."

I blinked. I don't know why I was surprised. Considering the size of the town, some of the locals had to be related.

"Oh, I didn't know that. Of course, that stands to reason," I said, leading into the next direction I intended to take the conversation. "Being new here, I don't really know much about anyone."

Walter laughed. "Yeah, that was clear when Ida Belle and

Gertie managed to rope you into their nonsense. Most people tend to stay out of their path when possible."

"Really? The way I hear it, Ida Belle practically runs Sinful."

"That's true enough." He looked upward. "Lord save us all from the machinations of an intelligent female."

I put my elbows on the counter and leaned toward Walter. "But *how* does she do it, exactly?"

He shrugged. "I do what she wants because I've been in love with her since elementary school. I don't know everyone else's reasons. Never asked."

The plot thickened. Either he was telling the truth, which I found charming, or he was lying.

Time for a different tactic. "I'm sure you heard we didn't find Marie on Number Two."

"I saw the long faces when you pulled up at the dock. I figured as much."

"What's the deal there? I gathered from Gertie and Ida Belle that Harvey wasn't well liked, but I don't get why everyone assumes Marie did it."

He narrowed his eyes at me. "So, let me get this straight—two strangers tell you they need your help finding a woman that they think killed her husband and who is hiding on a stinky island, and you thought it would be a good idea to go with them?"

I frowned. "When you put it that way, I guess it sounds a little sketchy."

"A little?" He shook his head. "You're not at all the way Marge described you. We were expecting some shrinking violet that looked down her nose at the bunch of hicks. The last thing I would have figured you for was hooking up with Ida Belle and Gertie and trying to protect a woman accused of murder."

"Marge and I weren't really close. I think she only knew

what Mother told her about me, and Mother tended to believe what she wanted and not what was reality. I don't know what to tell you, except that I guess I figured they were two nice, old ladies who needed help."

"Ha. Two nice, old ladies. I guess I can see how you would think so, not being from around here, but I'm guessing you've got a different opinion of their skill set by now."

"Yeah, but they seem good judges of character, and Marie was a friend of Marge's. I assume my aunt would be helping if she were alive, so I guess I figure it's the least I can do. Besides, Ida Belle and Gertie don't think Marie's dangerous, so why would I assume she is?"

Walter sighed. "She's probably not, and Marge definitely would have been in this up to her neck. To answer your earlier question, Harvey Chicoron was the biggest butthole this side of the Atchafalaya. But last time I checked, you couldn't kill a man for being an ass."

"That's sort of a shame, really," I said.

Walter raised his eyebrows. "Have anyone in mind?"

"Not at this moment, but give me some time."

"I'm beginning to get why Ida Belle enlisted your help."

I shook my head. "Looks like it's all for nothing. We haven't found hide nor hair of Marie, and as it seems everyone's sure of her guilt, I guess the outcome of this mess has already been determined. All that's left is the trial."

Walter nodded, his expression sad. "I'm afraid you're right, but no one in Sinful's going to be happy about it."

"Oh, that's not true. Harvey's cousin Melvin came to my house the other day, banging on the doors and windows and swearing I was harboring Marie. He somehow got it in his mind that I was her attorney. Tried to serve me with papers to keep her from spending her own money."

"Melvin's always been a useless cuss. Lazy as the day is long and always trying to get people to shell out money for his latest get-rich scheme. He couldn't get money off of Harvey, and that always hacked him off. It's probably been eating him alive that Marie's had control of Harvey's estate all these years."

"So, if Marie goes to prison, does Melvin get the money?"

"I've never heard anything about Harvey leaving a will. Sorta stupid for a rich man, but Harvey wasn't the brightest of bulbs. Far as I know, Melvin is next of kin, so I guess he'd come into it all."

I whistled. "Talk about hitting the lottery."

"Yep. It would be about the same thing."

"So, why don't people think Melvin killed Harvey?"

Walter frowned. "It's crossed my mind a time or two, but there's a couple things that keep me from latching onto that theory. First one is that unless Melvin could make certain Marie was blamed for Harvey's death, he still wouldn't benefit."

"That's true. And you don't think he's smart enough to do that?"

"Clearly not. If he did it, he kinda screwed up the finding-the-body part of the crime. You can't exactly convict Marie of killing her husband if no one can prove he's dead."

"But surely Harvey wouldn't have disappeared and left all the money behind."

"There was some rumors—I don't have any hard proof, mind you—that he was carrying on with a woman from New Orleans and they were planning to run off together. I've heard whispers that a good sum of money was missing from his accounts, but I can't get any details out of Carter."

That figured. "You said a couple of reasons...."

"Yeah, second one is that when Harvey disappeared, Melvin was sitting in prison in New Orleans."

"I don't suppose he could have had a friend do it—especially as he had the perfect alibi?"

"I don't know. Melvin didn't have any friends that I'm aware of, and besides which, where the heck has the body been all this time? If there was a plan in all this, it was botched big time."

I sighed. "I guess you're right. So there's no one else that might have taken a shot at Harvey?"

"Shoot—throw a stone and you'll hit someone who wanted to. There's no shortage of people who are happier in Sinful with no Harvey Chicoron. Hell, I'm one of them, but it's a big leap from hating a man to putting a bullet in him."

"Yeah, I suppose it is." *For normal people.*

Then I processed the rest of his statement. "*You*, Walter? You seem so calm. Why would you want to shoot him?"

"Harvey's family built and owned most of Main Street. Me, the butcher, the churches, and Francine all rented the space. We tried to buy it for years, but Harvey's parents wouldn't sell. Then Harvey got control when his parents died and decided to put the screws to everyone. He doubled the rent, and we either had to pay up or get out."

I shook my head. "I would have shot him for you if I'd been here."

"Normally, I'm a peaceful man, but I'd be lying if I didn't say it crossed my mind a lot more than once that everyone in this town would be better off if Harvey was dead."

"So when he disappeared, I guess that problem went away."

"Sure. First thing Marie did after she got control of the estate was lower the rent back to the old rate. Then she sold us our buildings at a more than fair price."

Walter narrowed his eyes at me. "What's your interest in all this, anyway? You one of them amateur sleuth sorts?"

"I find that sort of thing interesting." The lie rolled easily out of my mouth. "But I guess mostly I was hoping the answer was something else besides Marie. Seems like everyone likes her, and the more I hear about her, the more I like her myself."

"That's very true. It's going to be a sad day if Marie goes away for killing Harvey. Likely, ain't no one going to be happy about it but Melvin."

I nodded, and for some reason, my thoughts flashed back to the letters I'd found in Marge's attic. "Can I ask you something?"

Walter laughed. "You've already been asking me something for twenty minutes."

I smiled. "Okay. Can I ask you something else?"

"As I don't get much opportunity to talk to young, beautiful women, you can stay here talking as long as you want."

"There're a lot of older, single people in this town—Ida Belle and Gertie, Marge, you. What's the deal? No offense, but you're in an age group that usually settled down for the whole kids-golden-retriever-and-white-picket-fence thing."

"Ida Belle, Gertie and your aunt were feminists ahead of their time. Can't really blame them for wanting more than the role society told them they was supposed to fill. I'm not much for being told what to do, either."

"Me, either. So, my aunt never had a romance with anyone?"

He frowned and shook his head. "Not that I can recall, although I often wondered if she didn't meet someone in Vietnam."

"Why do you say that?"

"When she came back, she had that look sometimes...like she was thinking hard about someone that wasn't available. I know that feeling."

"Ida Belle?"

He nodded. "All my life, there's only been one woman for me. If I can't have her, then I don't want any other."

"Walter, you're an old romantic!"

He gave me a sheepish smile. "I suppose there's worse things to be."

———

GIVEN THE SIZE OF MY BREAKFAST, I PROBABLY SHOULD HAVE jogged home, but I didn't have the energy. Instead, I shuffled back to the house, loaded down with bags. Walter had helped me stock up on plenty of easy-to-prepare food and had assured me the battery for the Jeep was on its way. Then he'd given me a free bottle of Sinful Ladies cough syrup and a wink before I'd headed out. I decided Ida Belle could do a whole lot worse than settling down with Walter.

As I walked, my mind ran through everything that had happened since I'd arrived in Sinful. As much as I hadn't wanted to care, I found myself drawn to the mystery surrounding Harvey Chicoron's death, everyone's presumption that Marie was the perpetrator, and the equally consistent belief that Harvey had deserved it and no one wanted Marie to pay.

I almost felt sorry for the prosecuting attorney, but then the attorney part kept getting in the way of complete sympathy after the dealings I'd had with them. Still, they were in for some serious anger issues from the Sinful population when it came trial time. Except for Melvin. That idiot would probably be in court every day holding up a sign that read, MARIE DID IT, if the judge allowed such things.

My search for an alternative suspect was leading nowhere fast. I'd had hopes that talking to Walter might yield another angle, but apparently, the most likely people to have popped off Harvey, besides Marie, were the pastor, the priest, the butcher, Francine, and Walter.

I sighed. The more I learned about Harvey, the more I wondered if everyone's assumption of Marie's guilt was a bit of a leap. It seemed that a number of people had very valid reasons for wanting him out of the way.

My imagination was still whirling with all the insane possibilities for a suspect when I looked around and realized I'd walked right past my house. Good grief. I needed some serious work on my focus. Someone could have capped me right there on the sidewalk, and I wouldn't even have seen them coming.

I trudged up to the house and breathed a sigh of relief when I jiggled the front door and found it locked. At least Sinful hadn't eaten away all of my survival instincts.

Bones was awake for a change and standing at the back door. I took that to mean it was break time and opened the back door to let him saunter out. As it was a nice day and the kitchen knives were in easy reach, I left the door open so he could come back in whenever he was done with whatever one-hundred-year-old hound dogs did when they weren't digging up bodies.

In the time it took me to pour myself a glass of soda, he'd already shuffled back in and climbed back into his bed in the corner. For one who'd started all this flurry, *he* didn't seem to have any problem sleeping. By my estimation, he managed a good twenty-three hours of sleep out of any twenty-four-hour day.

I closed and locked the back door, then tackled the supply bags. It took only a couple of minutes to unpack the groceries; then I wandered around the downstairs of the house for a bit, trying to find something to do. After my fourth pass around the living room, I flopped into a recliner and blew out a breath.

I was bored.

For the first time since I'd arrived in Sinful, I was finally getting a dose of that whole slower-pace thing. Unless you had sleeping habits like Bones, it wasn't all it was cracked up to be. I pondered for a moment what it said about me exactly that I'd rather be risking my cover by getting involved in the investigation of a murder committed by a woman I'd never met to a husband that no one liked, than taking a nap.

It took only a minute to decide I wasn't cut out for a slower pace. This bit of excitement was probably the first Sinful had seen since Harvey went missing, so I supposed I ought to be grateful for the timing as it had given me some distraction. Technically, I supposed I should be cataloging the stuff in Marge's house and packing it for sale, but that seemed even more boring than just sitting here.

I pulled my cell phone from my pocket and checked the display for the tenth time since entering the house. No calls. No messages. Maybe Ida Belle and Gertie were taking a day off. That would be about right—as soon as I got knee-deep in it all, they were taking a step back.

I gazed up at the picture on the fireplace mantel that Gertie had identified as Marge and Marie. They were on Main Street and both smiling. Streamers hung from light posts, so there must have been some sort of celebration going on. The photo next to it was one of Marge with a group of men standing next to a giant dead deer. They were all dressed in camouflage and looked to be having the time of their lives.

The picture reminded me of Marge's military uniforms lumped on the desk upstairs, so I hopped up from the chair and headed to the bedroom. I didn't like those uniforms being rumpled. This was the perfect opportunity to iron them and get them back into the shape they were meant to be in. Ironing wasn't exactly my favorite thing to do, but it was better than sitting there, and restoring the uniforms to pristine state would provide a certain level of satisfaction that I hadn't really achieved since landing in Sinful.

I retrieved the ironing board and iron I'd seen in the spare room across from the one I was using, then set up in front of the window in my own room. The light was nice, and it afforded me a great view of the street.

I hunted down starch in the kitchen pantry while the iron was heating up, then picked the first set of pants and jacket off the table and went to work. Normally, you couldn't find me doing anything domestic, but ironing was different. Growing up with a former military commander as a father tended to lend itself to good grooming. He'd even insisted on ironing sheets and underwear.

Of course, as soon as I left home, I abandoned all that nonsense, but couldn't give up the ghost on military uniforms. Sometimes something was simply the right thing to do. Armed with my starch and a hot iron, I went to work on the jacket.

When I finished pressing the jacket to within an inch of perfection, I stood there holding it for a moment, thinking it was a real shame to fold such a beautifully ironed garment. Maybe I should hang up the uniforms. A museum or collector might be interested in them. You never knew what people were interested in having.

I'd used all the hangers in the guest room for my own wardrobe, the vast majority of which I hadn't bothered to wear, so I went in search of more. The closets in the other spare rooms contained only neatly stacked and labeled storage boxes, so I went to dig through the closet in the master bedroom.

It was a large walk-in with clothes rods on each side and shelves above. Marge's clothes were arranged according to type and color. No surprise there after seeing her pantry. A bunch of empty hangers dangled from the rod at the back of the closet, so I snagged a handful of them.

Apparently, my mind overreached my grasp because I lost my grip and they popped out of my hand and onto the closet floor. Sighing, I leaned over to gather up the hangers. I reached for the last one and pulled, but it appeared to be stuck on something. I tugged harder and heard a faint click.

A second later, the back panel of the closet slid back, revealing a wall of weapons that made me gasp.

Holy crap!

Pistols, rifles, semi-automatic, full automatic, knives, swords, grenades...I felt my heart pounding, and I got a bit short of breath. What a beautiful, beautiful collection. I ran my fingers reverently over a grenade launcher I'd been coveting for months. Marge had seriously good taste.

Clearly Deputy LeBlanc didn't know anything about Marge's hidden stash. He'd removed a bunch of hunting rifles and a pistol and left all the good stuff behind.

I pulled an assault rifle from the wall and inspected it. It was in perfect operating condition. What the hell had Marge done in the military to warrant this level of interest in weapons? I knew she was a hunter, but this was hardly the type of gun one used to bag a deer.

I put the rifle back on its hanger and reached for an excellent nine millimeter. The clip was full and it was a beauty. Certainly, Marge wouldn't mind my borrowing her gun while I was visiting. I stuck it in my waistband, then squatted to feel the panel where the hanger was lodged. Sure enough, there was a little switch under the edge of the baseboard. I moved the hanger out of the way and pressed the switch. The panel slid silently back in place.

Whatever she was up to, apparently Marge felt it necessary to keep her collection under wraps. I couldn't imagine something like this remaining a secret for long if someone among the general Sinful populace knew about it. And if it hadn't been a secret, Deputy LeBlanc would definitely have removed all the guns from the house after she died.

I smiled as I walked back to my bedroom with a handful of hangers, the pistol tucked nicely at my waist. I heard a boat cruising down the bayou behind the house and two birds land on a tree outside—all without casting a glance out a window. Amazing how one good pistol made all the difference in a person. I was starting to feel normal again.

What Deputy LeBlanc didn't know wouldn't hurt him.

CHAPTER SIXTEEN

AFTER IRONING ALL THE UNIFORMS, I SPENT A GOOD CHUNK of the afternoon drooling over Marge's weapon collection and then took a nice, long nap before slumping onto the couch and cruising through hours of bad television. No one called, banged on the door, or dug up bones in my yard, and I was really starting to long for some excitement.

I almost wept with relief when my cell phone rang at nine p.m., and I saw Gertie's name on the display.

"I got a line on Melvin," Gertie said. "We'll pick you up in five."

She hung up before I could do anything rational like ask where we were going, or even smarter, refuse to go.

I jumped up from the couch and ran upstairs for my shoes. Who was I kidding? Like it or not, the situation intrigued me, and at the moment, I was more afraid of being bored to death than discovered by a Middle Eastern hit squad. Besides, it would give me great pleasure to find Marie before Deputy LeBlanc and come up with a viable alternative to Harvey's murderer.

As I came down the stairs and back into the living room, I

saw headlights flash across the front window and heard a car pull into the drive. I knew immediately that the low purr was not Gertie's ancient Cadillac. I stepped outside and stopped short at the sight of the black, sexy Corvette idling in my driveway.

The passenger window went down and Gertie waved her arm at me. "Hurry up, already."

I locked the door and hurried over as Gertie climbed out and motioned me into the car. I stuck one foot inside the car and twisted my body into a pretzel, then glided onto the center console and partially unraveled. Gertie simply turned with her butt over the passenger's seat and dropped.

Ida Belle frowned. "You need to work out. Your knees wouldn't be in such bad shape if you'd exercise a bit."

"My knees wouldn't need to exercise if you'd get a car suitable for a woman your age. Damn thing sits nearly on the ground."

"This car is smoking hot," I said. "I would never have figured you for a Corvette woman."

"There're a lot of things you don't know about me," Ida Belle said, "but I'm about to tell you a couple of them. First off, this is my garage car, meaning I don't take it out very often, and I let people ride in it even less often than that. I have a truck I use for everyday stuff, but it's in the shop at the moment since I made the mistake of letting *someone* borrow it."

Gertie pretended to study her seat belt.

Ida Belle continued. "And since Gertie turned her Cadillac into a swimming pool and now it stinks to high heaven, I had no choice but to use my baby as this is an emergency."

She turned and pointed her finger at me, then Gertie, glaring at both of us. "But if either of you so much as puts a scratch or dent on this car, I will shoot you and leave the body for the gators."

I nodded and wisely kept my mouth shut. As I'd recently been made aware of Ida Belle's shooting acumen, I figured it was best to treat the car like fine china.

Gertie nodded, but as soon as Ida Belle turned around, she looked back at me and rolled her eyes.

"So, I take it you heard from Myrtle?" I asked, as Ida Belle pulled out of the driveway and drove toward Main Street.

"Yep," Gertie said. "She gave us the names of Melvin's cell-mates while he was inside. He had three different ones, but two were still there with him when Harvey disappeared."

"And the third?"

"Killed in a car wreck the day after he was paroled."

"And I take it that Harvey was still alive and kicking then?"

"Unfortunately, yes."

Another dead end. I glanced out the window and realized we'd driven right through downtown Sinful and were now on a lonely stretch of highway in the middle of the marsh. "So, then, where are we going?"

"Ida Belle figured that since Melvin showed up to serve you papers," Gertie said, "he was itching to get his hands on the money. He must have had everything ready to go if Harvey's body was discovered. No way Melvin got anything done that fast or without help. He's just not that smart."

Ida Belle nodded. "So I figured if we could find him associating with some nefarious character that was available to kill Harvey back then, we'd have our suspect."

I groaned. "Please don't tell me we're on our way to some place with an abundance of nefarious characters."

Gertie clapped her hands. "We're going to the Swamp Bar. I've never been."

Oh no. "The place where you sent Deputy LeBlanc running off to yesterday?"

"One and the same." Gertie gave me an approving look. "I'm glad you wore black. I didn't think to mention it."

"They have a dress code?"

"No. We can't actually go *in* the bar. Too many of the regulars don't like Ida Belle."

"Should I even ask why?"

Ida Belle shrugged. "It's just some nonsense over the shooting competition at the annual fair."

Gertie nodded. "The nonsense part being that Ida Belle whups their butts every year."

"Of course she does," I muttered. "So, if we can't go inside, what's the plan?"

"We're going to park at the end of the parking lot, where it's easiest to make a getaway, and then peek in the windows." Gertie almost squealed. "And I can get some pictures with my phone. Those phone pictures have been right handy."

"This is exciting to you?" I asked. "Sneaking around in a swamp to spy on nefarious characters? I've got to tell you, I tried that whole sneaking around thing in the suburbs, and it didn't work out so well, especially for Deputy LeBlanc's hamburgers. I'm pretty sure sneaking in the swamp is an even worse idea."

"You worry a lot, dear," Gertie said. "It's really not good for your health."

I sighed. Of all the things I'd done in my life, worrying was the least of the things I'd done to affect my health.

"The most important thing to remember," Ida Belle said, "is to remove your shoes before getting back in the car. I've tucked some trash bags in the trunk."

Unbelievable. With everything they had planned, Ida Belle's biggest worry was getting the car dirty. I was more concerned that something besides our shoes would get shoved into those trash bags and thrown in the trunk at the end of the night.

My unrest increased tenfold as Ida Belle turned off the paved highway and onto a road comprised entirely of dirt and shells that seemed to lead directly into the heart of the swamp.

She decreased her speed to barely above an idle, and I could hear the shells crunching under the tires. I hoped to God that if we ran into trouble, Ida Belle cared more about saving our butts than saving her paint job.

The further we progressed, the narrower the road became, or maybe it was just that the brush got thicker and closer to the road. Either way, combined with the pitch-black sky and complete lack of light except for the headlights of the car, it gave me a feeling of claustrophobia and being lost in a vast desert all at the same time. Normally, such things wouldn't bother me. I'd dismiss feelings as counterproductive to the mission and move on, but ever since I'd arrived in Louisiana, I'd felt off balance. Oddly enough, foreign countries felt more familiar than this stretch of the U.S.

Finally, I saw a tiny flicker of light in the middle of the black. As we drew closer, the faint lines of the large building came into view. It was comprised of weathered wood—rotted in places—and a tin roof with holes rusted through it. I completely understood Francine's sentiment about decent women not coming out here for a drink. I wouldn't walk in the place unless I had two guns pulled and an up-to-date tetanus shot.

Ida Belle backed her car into a stretch of dirt at the far end of the open space that served as a parking lot. A truck with giant wheels blocked it completely from view of anyone in the bar—anyone that could see in the dark, that is.

I unfolded myself out of the car and looked at my two partners in crime. "Well?"

"We thought you'd need a moment for the blood flow to return to your legs," Gertie explained. She looked over at Ida Belle. "She's in really good shape."

Ida Belle waved a hand in dismissal. "Let's get this done. It's going to take me the rest of the night to get those bugs off my paint job, and I still have to roll my hair."

"There's Melvin's truck," I said, pointing to the rust bucket I'd seen him peel away from my house in.

"Good," Ida Belle said. "Then this isn't a waste of time."

I didn't bother to respond. The jury was still *way* out on that one.

We started across the open patch toward the building, and I immediately saw a problem. "Where are the windows?"

I had a clear view of the front and one side of the building. The side with the door in the center had a porch light, but there wasn't a window in sight, and no glow emitted out of the walls.

"Too much glass in a place like this is dangerous," Ida Belle explained. "There're window openings on the bayou side that they cover with plywood when they close the bar."

Nice. "Seems a lot of effort. What time do they close?"

"I think the last time was in 1982."

"Uh-huh. What about during Katrina?"

"No way! It was dollar-beer night."

I knew I was going to regret it, but I couldn't help but ask. "So, what *did* manage to close the bar?"

"AC/DC was performing in New Orleans. The brothers that own the bar are huge fans, and neither would agree to stay behind and keep the bar open. Normally, it wouldn't be a problem as their father would have filled in, but he was in jail at the time for shooting one of the patrons."

Yep. I regretted it.

"Is Father Shooter still around?"

"Yeah, he's the bouncer, but his vision's going, so it's unlikely he'd hit you if he got off a shot."

"Unlikely" didn't seem all that great of odds, but this was my penance for not asking for specifics before getting into Ida Belle's car. If I managed to get through this unscathed, I was going to start requiring them to complete a detailed description of the mission—in writing—before I agreed to anything else.

"All segues into eighties rock bands and murder two aside, how exactly are we supposed to peek inside the bar if the only windows are over the bayou?"

"We're going to steal a boat, of course," Gertie said.

"Of course we are," I grumbled. I don't know why I'd asked. It should have been so obvious. "And if someone sees us?"

"Oh, wait!" Gertie reached into her enormous handbag and pulled out three black ski masks. "This will hide our identities."

I didn't bother to point out that the options for three people —two old, one young—who would steal a boat at the Swamp Bar to spy on someone, wouldn't be that hard to pick out of the Sinful population. I pulled on the ski mask. What the hell.

I looked over at Ida Belle and Gertie and winced. Black ski masks, black sweats, and black turtlenecks were definitely not the happening thing for senior citizens. Ida Belle pointed to the left and started walking. I followed the two thieving seniors to the pier and stared into the dim glow cast by the pier light, studying our options. All of them looked like they were five seconds away from following the Titanic down, and I'd be willing to bet none of them had Leonardo DiCaprio, or anyone remotely resembling him, on board.

"The one on the end is best," Ida Belle said. "It will be quieter and easier."

Both good things when you're stealing, I supposed.

"Okay," Ida Belle instructed, "you guys take the boat around. I'm going to circle the bar and keep watch from the bank on the back side."

"You're leaving me alone with Gertie in the boat?" I asked. "What glasses is she wearing?"

"She's only got to go ten feet. *That* she can manage. But just in case, do you want the person with the only set of car keys on board with you?"

I sighed and stepped into the boat as Ida Belle disappeared into the darkness. Gertie stepped in and stopped to pick up a long pole from the bottom of the boat. She handed it to me, then grabbed an oar and went to the back of the boat.

"Stick the pole in the water and use it to push the boat," she said. "I don't want to risk using the motor."

Because I agreed with her one hundred percent on that risk, I stuck the pole in the slimy mud at the bottom of the bayou and got to pushing. As we inched up to the side of the bar, I realized that quite literally half of it was perched on giant stilts right over the water. Waves of cigarette smoke billowed out the openings that served as windows, and I could already feel my lungs constricting. Loud country music blared from a jukebox, and I could hear the sounds of at least one fight.

But before we even got into position below the window, I could already see a problem. The window was a good foot above my head, even though I was standing on the bow.

"Darn it," Gertie said as she grabbed a knot on a piece of siding to hold us in place. "The tide's out."

"Is there anything I can stand on?"

Gertie brightened. "That's right! You have that catlike balance. There's a plastic bucket back here. Will that do?"

"That's fine," I grumbled, just wanting to get this over with.

"Hurry up!" Ida Belle hissed from around the corner on the bank.

I positioned the white bucket upside down on the bow and carefully stepped up onto it in a crouching position. Gertie passed me her smart phone, and I slowly rose up the side of the bar until I could peer inside.

The smoke was so thick, I had to wait for a good breeze to waft in before I could see much. I scanned the bar looking for that idiot Melvin, and finally spotted him sitting at a corner table, in deep conversation with a woman.

I squinted, trying to get a better look at her, but finally decided I hadn't seen her before.

"Do you see him?" Gertie whispered.

"Yeah. He's talking to a woman."

Five foot five, a hundred fifty pounds, probably good in a bar fight.

"She's a bit younger than him," I continued, "but rough around the edges. Really rough."

"It figures. We're trying to get a cover for Marie, and he's trying to get laid. Well, get a shot of them anyway. You never know what might come in handy."

I stuck the smart phone over the ledge and zoomed in on Melvin and his honey. I snapped a couple of pictures of them before he rose from the table and walked toward the counter.

"He's headed over to the bar. Maybe I can get a shot of him talking to someone else."

"We'll work with whatever you can get."

Melvin slid onto a stool at the bar and motioned to the bartender, a burly man that even I wouldn't want to take on in close quarters.

Six foot four, two hundred fifty pounds of mean.

I'd beat him in a footrace, hands down, but something told me he'd probably close that gap with a gun. The bartender filled two mugs of beer and slid them in front of Melvin. He leaned across the bar to speak to the bartender, who moved in so that they were only inches from each other.

I snapped a couple of pictures. That bartender was a great suspect. He was scary looking, of sketchy legal background, and had no reason to be sharing secrets with Melvin, especially as he'd already served the beer.

"Are you done yet?" Ida Belle hissed again. "More cars are

pulling up. We need to get out of here."

"Just a bit more," I said as I lowered the smart phone and watched Melvin as he left the counter. If he stopped to talk to anyone else on his way across the bar, I could get another shot.

The delay proved to be my undoing.

A slutty redhead with more cleavage showing than I'd seen in public in years, came walking into the bar. Melvin's head yanked around to get a better look as if it had been snapped with a rubber band; then he walked right into the back of an enormous bald guy's chair and dumped an entire mug of beer on top of him.

The guy sprang up, breaking the wooden chair in two with the effort, and clocked Melvin before he could even stutter out an apology. Three other men jumped in the fray, and it flashed across my mind that now was a good time to get the hell out of there.

"Bar fight," I said and tossed Gertie the smart phone.

I took one final peek inside just as the bartender stepped from behind the counter. The fight had ventured close to the window, and it was clear that Melvin was not going to come out on top of this one as he was currently curled in a ball on the floor. I looked back up just in time to see the bartender heave a bucket toward the fighters, and a second later, a burst of ice water hit me full in the face.

"What the hell!" the bartender yelled.

Through blurry eyes, I saw he'd locked in on me.

"Go!" I yelled at Gertie, but she was already ahead of me, tugging on the motor.

Before I could even jump off the bucket, the motor fired and she launched the boat backward, pitching me off into the bayou.

"Swim!" Ida Belle yelled from the bank as Gertie continued her backward run, showing no sign of slowing.

The front door to the bar burst open, and I heard people

running outside as I swam like an Olympic athlete for the bank. The cries of the outraged bar patrons echoed through the open swamp.

"Someone's stealing my boat!"

"Get 'em!"

"Grab my rifle!"

"Some bitch!"

As soon as my hands touched ground, I sprang up and ran as fast as the quicksand mud would allow. Ida Belle was standing in a patch of moonlight, gesturing frantically. We ran behind the row of cars and hurried down the edge of the marsh until we reached Ida Belle's car.

"They're all chasing Gertie," Ida Belle said as she unlocked her trunk. "Now's our chance to get out of here."

She reached into the trunk and tossed me a couple of trash bags. "Shed those clothes."

I stared. "You're serious?"

"Get naked, or I leave you here, but leave the mask on in case we run into anyone on the road home." She tossed me a towel. "Wipe the mud off your hands."

I could hear the search party mounting in size and temperament, but Ida Belle just stood there, not about to unlock the car doors. Refusing to die in the middle of the swamp at the hands of people who were not worthy opponents taken individually, I pulled off my clothes and shoved them in the trash bag, then wrapped the second trash bag around me.

Ida Belle finally unlocked the doors, and I jumped into the passenger's seat as she tossed the dirty clothes into the trunk. A couple seconds later, she slid into the driver's seat and we took off, sans headlights. Good God.

"For heaven's sake," Ida Belle complained, "don't touch anything. And keep your feet firmly in the middle of the floor mat."

I felt my back tighten as she drifted the Corvette around a

corner that I couldn't even see, praying there was road beneath us. "You have serious issues. You know that, right?"

"So you say, but my car doesn't smell like an algae bloom."

"What about Gertie? Aren't we going to help her?"

"Gertie's fine. She knows these channels like the back of her hand. She'll get away clean and leave the boat drifting."

Gertie's unadmitted vision problems made that seem far less of a sure thing than Ida Belle made it sound, but I was in no position to argue. I was in no position to do anything but get indoors.

"Uh-oh," Ida Belle said. "We've got company."

I turned around in my seat, but couldn't see anything behind us but the light from the bar.

"Not there," Ida Belle said.

I turned back around and saw headlights curving through the swamp ahead of us. "I guess there's no chance they're on a different road."

"There's only one road out here."

"Just stay cool," I said. "They're probably headed to the bar and will drive right past."

"You're probably right," Ida Belle said, but she didn't sound convinced.

But even as I said it, I knew we were sunk. "I don't suppose there are any more Corvettes in town...."

"Of course. Why do you think I chose American over a German model? Granted, mine is in much better shape, but all the drug dealers have black Corvettes. At night, I blend."

I didn't even bother to question the logic of blending with drug dealers. At the moment, it was a better option than being mistaken for ourselves. I held my breath as we rounded a corner that put us face-to-face with the other vehicle, which was stopped in the middle of the road, leaving no room to drive around.

Ida Belle slowed to a stop. "This is *so* not good."

I started to reach for my gun, then remembered my gun was in a trash bag in the trunk and probably waterlogged, anyway.

Someone rapped on my car window and I jumped. Ida Belle lowered the window and Deputy LeBlanc leaned down to look into the car. He didn't seem surprised to see either of us —and I had no doubt he knew who we were despite the masks —but his eyes widened when he saw my latest choice of garments.

He sighed. "I promised myself when I saw this car, that no matter what, I wasn't going to ask questions I really didn't want to know the answer to. But I have to admit, this one has tempted me beyond all good common sense."

"She fell into the bayou," Ida Belle said. "And she's not riding in my car in wet clothes, so I made her improvise. Give me a ticket if you want."

"And you fell in the bayou how, exactly?" he asked me.

"Trying to avoid a bar fight," I replied. It was the truth. The short version, anyway.

"Uh-huh. And why were you at the Swamp Bar to begin with?"

"Checking out the local culture."

"Do you always check out the local culture wearing ski masks?"

"We did facials before we left my house," Ida Belle chimed in. "This is supposed to make us look ten years younger."

"I see. So your visit wouldn't have anything to do with the fact that Melvin usually hangs out at the Swamp Bar when he's not in jail."

"Really?" Ida Belle said. "I had no idea, but then, we weren't there long."

He snorted. "I bet. Where's your partner in crime?"

"Gertie has a headache and stayed home to rest," Ida Belle said.

Deputy LeBlanc raised an eyebrow. "So, if I called her house right now, she'd answer?"

"Of course not. I told you she was resting."

"Uh-huh. Then she wouldn't know anything about the call I got concerning a stolen boat..."

"Not unless she's psychic," I volunteered.

Deputy LeBlanc closed his eyes for a moment, and I could see him mentally counting to ten. Finally, he opened his eyes and pointed at Ida Belle. "Turn on your headlights, take off those ridiculous masks, drive straight home, and do not come out of your house for the rest of the night. If you were a decent, kind person, I'd tell you to stay inside your house for an entire day so that I could catch a break, but I'm not going to waste my breath."

"And you," he said to me, "if you're going to continue hanging out with these two—against good advice, I might add —then at least carry a change of clothes. I've seen you in more states of undress than I did my last girlfriend."

Ida Belle rolled up the window, probably saving me from a retort I could ill afford, given the circumstances. Deputy LeBlanc walked back to his truck and backed up to let Ida Belle pull past him.

"Headlights!" he yelled as we drove past.

Ida Belle pulled off her mask and flipped on her headlights, creeping down the rock road. I pulled off my mask, and my skin screamed with relief to have the sticky, wet fabric no longer clinging to it. As soon as we hit the highway, Ida Belle launched the Corvette down the road at a clip so fast it had me gripping the sides of the seat.

She glanced down at my hands. "I told you not to touch anything, you pansy."

I released the seat and glared. "You and I have to talk. As soon as I have regular clothes on and am strapped with a weapon."

Ida Belle opened her mouth to retort, but her cell phone rang, interrupting whatever she was about to say, which given my current mood, was probably a really good thing for Ida Belle.

"It's Gertie," Ida Belle said to me as she answered the phone.

"Where are you?" Ida Belle asked.

I held my breath waiting for the answer, but Ida Belle only mumbled a few times.

"Meet us at Marge's," she barked into the phone and disconnected.

"Well?" I asked.

"She's about to hop in the shower and will meet us at your place."

"Her own shower?"

"No, she's showering with some hot guy she met on the boat ride home. Of course her own shower."

I shook my head. Here I was naked, wearing a trash bag, and facing another twenty minutes of this humiliation, and the senior citizen boat thief was hopping in a nice hot shower. So many things were wrong about this, I didn't even have the mental faculties to list them all.

I rode in absolute silence the rest of the way home. It was best not to let my thoughts out into the atmosphere. Gertie opened the front door, holding a fresh cup of coffee. I walked right past her without a word and went straight upstairs for a shower and clothes. With any luck, they'd take a hint and leave while I was gone, but when I went downstairs fifteen minutes later, they were eating the chocolate pie I'd bought from Walter and drinking coffee.

When I walked into the room, they stopped talking. Gertie looked at me while Ida Belle looked at her coffee. Then Gertie kicked Ida Belle under the table and she lifted her gaze to mine.

"I'm sorry I made you ride naked in my car wearing a trash bag," she said, not sounding the least bit sorry.

"No, you're not," I said. "And furthermore, do you really think a simple apology can make up for Deputy LeBlanc seeing me in that state?"

Gertie sucked in a breath and stared at Ida Belle in horror. "You didn't tell me that part."

"Of course she didn't. That part makes her look really bad, not to mention gives the whole shooting match away to Deputy LeBlanc as, likely, no one else at the Swamp Bar was soaking wet immediately after a boat was stolen."

Gertie frowned at Ida Belle, shaking her head. "You have got to get over that car or sell it. It makes you crazy."

"Oh, she's fine with the car where I'm concerned," I said. "There could be a Cat 5 hurricane headed this way, and even if it was the only vehicle in town, I wouldn't set foot in it again."

"I don't blame her," Gertie said.

Ida Belle threw her hands up in the air. "Fine! I'm sorry. I wasn't trying to embarrass anyone or get us caught. I'll work on my car issues."

Because she finally looked a tiny bit contrite, Gertie nodded and I poured a cup of coffee and sat down.

"I put your clothes in to wash," Gertie said. "But you'll need to move them to the dryer. Don't forget. With the humidity down here, they'll get to smelling quickly."

Another glorious trait of Louisiana.

I took a drink of coffee. "Please tell me we got something out of all of this."

"Oh yes," Gertie said, her frown vanishing.

"Good. That bartender is a scary-looking guy. I figured he would make a good target for us."

Gertie shook her head. "Oh, no. Not the bartender."

I frowned. "The woman?"

"Not just any woman. That's Marie's third cousin, Cheryl."

Ida Belle nodded. "A nasty piece of trash that got run out of Sinful years ago. She was always jealous of Marie."

"Okay. But assuming she had opportunity and slight motive, we still have to prove means. And how would she have colluded with Melvin while he was locked up?"

"That's the best part." Gertie smiled. "She's a prison guard."

I stared. "At Melvin's prison?"

"Yep. How cool is that?"

My mind raced with the possibilities. "Okay, this is good. It's really good. Please tell me the picture I took is clear."

"Clear as a bell," Gertie said. "We're in business. Well, except for one small thing."

Ida Belle narrowed her eyes at Gertie. "What small thing?"

"I think Melvin might have seen me. I couldn't drive the boat with the mask on. The spotlight only hit me for a second, and I ducked, but he was standing on the end of the pier."

Ida Belle frowned.

"Do you think he'll retaliate?" I asked.

"I don't think so," Ida Belle said. "He's stupid, that's certain, but he's got no reason to suspect we're trying to frame him for murder. Even if he knows we were there spying on him, what's the harm from his point of view?"

"True," I agreed, although I would have felt better if Melvin had remained ignorant of it all.

"We did it!" Gertie said, clapping her hands.

"Sure," I said, "just as soon as we find Marie, she gets arrested, and we find her an attorney, we can give them our theory and the picture."

Gertie's face fell a bit. "Maybe there's a bit more to do, but this is still a big piece of our plan."

"Yes," I agreed. "It's a big piece."

"Now," Ida Belle said, "we just need to find Marie."

I blew out a breath. Yeah, *just*.

CHAPTER SEVENTEEN

AFTER ALL THE EXCITEMENT, THE HOT SHOWER, AND THE pie, I should have been able to drop off to sleep, but no matter how many times I tossed around in the bed, it just didn't seem to happen. Maybe it had been too much excitement, or more likely, too much coffee, but either way, sleep did not come. Finally, I decided I'd grab my book and read myself into slumber.

I jumped out of bed and headed over to the desk, where I'd left my book that afternoon. As I reached for it, I knocked the stack of envelopes containing Marge's unmailed letters onto the floor. The rubber band broke against the hardwood floor and they scattered.

Sighing, I bent over to pick them up. As I reached for one that had slid under the edge of the bed, I saw pen marks on the front of the envelope that none of the others had. I straightened up and studied the marks. It was some sort of drawing, but didn't look like anything recognizable. Then I realized I was holding the envelope upside down. When I turned it around, it was all too clear.

It was a sketch of a woman's face. Clean simple lines, no

bigger than a quarter. And a single tear on the woman's cheek. I stacked the rest of the envelopes on the desk and crawled in bed with my book and the envelope with the drawing, wondering if this one was different for a reason.

I got my answer as soon as I started to read.

I GOT THE NEWS FROM FRANCINE. YOU ARE TO BE MARRIED. I knew someone like you would not live their life out alone, but it is like a knife through my heart. Why, Harvey? The pain I feel is almost unbearable.

Nothing matters any longer. Not the war or even my return.

In two months, I will be in Sinful for the first time in two years, but I'll be alone.

At least here in the jungle, I have a purpose. I have people to take care of. I have important work to do.

I fear my reaction when I see you together for the first time on Main Street. I wonder how I'll live there the rest of my life with you just out of my grasp and in the arms of someone else.

I LET OUT A GASP AS I READ.

Harvey?

The man that Marge had pined for and written all those unmailed letters to was Harvey Chicoron—the biggest asshole in the state?

Dumbfounded, I flopped back on my pillow. This changed everything. If Marge had carried unrequited love for Harvey all these years, watched him marry Marie, and then seen him take up affairs with most of the women in the parish, God only knows what she'd felt.

What she'd planned.

I sucked in a breath. Could she really have loved him so much she killed him? Surely love didn't work that way—not real love. But maybe, all the years of being pushed aside for someone prettier or younger or more pliable had turned all that overwhelming love into something else—something dark.

God knows, Marge had the weaponry to take him out, and her military experience had provided the skill to use it. Could she have really taken things that far over a man who beat her friend and slept with everything with a pulse?

And how many other people knew about Marge's feelings for Harvey? Surely Ida Belle and Gertie didn't, or they would have suggested Marge as an option for the murder in the first place. They might not like incriminating a friend, but in this case, the friend was long past this world and couldn't be hurt by the accusation.

Still, if Marge had managed to keep her crush on Harvey a secret from Gertie, Ida Belle, and most importantly, Marie, then she must have been the best actress the world had ever seen.

I stared out the window into the pitch-black night and shook my head. How could such complicated things go on in such a small place? I never would have imagined it could be so. I'd always gone out of my way to streamline my life—removing all potential complication. I suddenly realized that mostly meant not having people around. Clearly, people were the biggest complication life threw at you.

I slipped the letter back in the envelope and placed it on the nightstand. Letting out a sigh, I turned off the lamp and slid down in the cool sheets, trying to redirect my mind's focus on anything but my own life. Since coming to Sinful, I'd already taken one too many uncomfortable looks inside myself. I wasn't sure I could take another revelation without a good night's sleep.

I had just dozed off when I bolted upright.

There was scuffling in the attic!

I hopped out of bed and hurried over to the bag of supplies

I'd gotten from the general store. That furry little rodent wasn't getting the best of me this time. I was prepared with a spotlight and pellet pistol, both acquisitions from the general store. Walter didn't have to run a background check on those, and they wouldn't damage the roof.

Armed with my legally acquired weapons, I crept up the attic stairs and paused a minute, allowing my eyes to adjust to the darkness. A thin stream of moonlight filtered through the attic window, casting a dim glow across the cluttered room.

I scanned it left and right, but didn't see any sign of my furry intruder. I heard a faint scratching noise behind a row of boxes at the back of the attic, and eased across the floor, carefully testing and choosing the floorboards that felt less likely to creak. Just a couple more steps and I'd have the varmint in my sights.

One, two, three...

I leapt over the row of boxes, clicking on the spotlight as I jumped. The light pierced through the darkness of the attic and lit it up like an explosion. I blinked once to get a visual in the glaring light, then leveled my pellet pistol at the scraping noise in the corner.

"Don't shoot!" a female voice sounded in front of me.

Startled, I dropped the spotlight and it crashed to the floor, pointing the beam of light behind me. I looked back into the shadows as a figure emerged, fully expecting one of the Sinful Ladies to fess up to doing God knows what under orders from Ida Belle or Gertie. Then I stared in shock.

"Marie!"

There was no doubt in my mind it was her. Despite her age, her face hadn't changed one bit from the photographs I'd seen of her as a younger woman. She walked slowly toward me, her hands in the air.

I shoved the pellet pistol in my waistband. "What the hell

are you doing in my attic? And put your hands down. I'm not going to shoot you. I've been trying to find you."

She lowered her hands and nodded. "I know. I've heard you talking to Ida Belle and Gertie. The kitchen vents come right up into my hiding place."

"You've been hiding here all this time?" I asked, but even as the words left my mouth, I thought about Bones' constant attempts to walk up the stairs. I'd passed it off as senility or smelling the raccoon, but it had been Marie.

"You must have been miserable," I said as I lifted the spotlight from the floor.

"It's not that bad," she said and motioned to the corner behind me. I turned to find a rocking chair with a stack of knitting and some books next to it. A military cot piled with blankets ran alongside the wall next to the chair.

"The boxes blocked off my cubby hole from clear view. I figured unless you really looked hard, you wouldn't realize..."

And I hadn't. Some intelligence agent.

The entire time I'd been traipsing through the swamp trying to find Marie, she'd been knitting right above me while I slept. I could almost feel my father frowning and was infinitely glad Director Morrow would never hear about my total lapse in concentration and ability.

"So, you set all this up when I was running around with Ida Belle and Gertie?"

"Not really. The cot and chair were already here. Marge suffered from a bit of PTSD. Sometimes she'd stay up here. I think it made her feel safe, like when she was in the military camp."

"Well, it was certainly a good place to hide. No one was looking for you here, that's for sure."

"Except for that situation with the raccoon, it's been fine. I knew all the places everyone would check. That's why I went to Number Two and left that blanket, hoping to throw people off track. I checked into a motel on the way to New Orleans on Saturday and paid for a week, just in case people were looking harder than Number Two."

I shook my head, still marveling that Marie had been in my attic the entire time. "But why? Why hide at all when it was only delaying the inevitable?"

Marie sighed. "I don't know. I know it was cowardly, but I didn't want to be put on the spot until I had a good story."

"But Ida Belle and Gertie would have helped you."

"And gotten themselves in hot water for doing it. No, I needed to figure out a plan myself, and I wasn't going to be able to do that sitting in jail or being stalked by that idiot Melvin."

"So, did you come up with something?"

The sadness was apparent in her expression as she shook her head.

"Well, you may as well come downstairs. You've got a lot of explaining to do, and I'm going to have to call Ida Belle and Gertie. They've been worried for too long already. I figure all this calls for coffee."

"And maybe a shot of whiskey?"

"Definitely."

We tromped downstairs to the living room, where Bones was standing at the bottom of the stairs, wagging his tail. I hadn't seen him so animated since he'd dug up the bone. Marie stopped to scratch behind his ears, and he licked her arm. He looked up at me, and I swear, there was a clear "I told you so" in his expression. He turned and trudged back to his bed in the kitchen and was snoring before we even walked in behind him.

I laid my weapon on the counter and pulled out coffee. Marie slumped into a chair at the breakfast table and sighed. She looked completely beat and more than a little worried, which made perfect sense given the situation, but I got the impression more was bothering her than what I knew.

"Is there anything you'd like to tell me...before we call Gertie and Ida Belle?"

Marie looked at me, trying for a casual expression and failing. "No. Why would there be?"

"Because you have this look like something is wrong besides the obvious."

"Well, there's an awful lot wrong. It would be strange if I didn't look worried."

I dumped grounds into the coffeemaker, poured in water and flipped the switch, then grabbed plates and forks and put them on the table next to what was left of the chocolate pie. At the rate it was going, it had been a good decision to buy three.

I studied Marie for a couple of seconds, and she shifted uncomfortably under my scrutiny. Finally, I took a seat across from her.

"It's not worry that I see. It's guilt."

Marie's eyes widened. "I don't have anything I should feel guilty about."

I smiled at her words. "I didn't say you *should* feel guilty. I said you do. But nice work dancing around that statement."

"I'm sure I don't know what you mean."

I cut off a slice of chocolate pie and placed it in front of Marie. "You didn't kill your husband, did you?"

"No."

"But you know who did."

She sighed. "Not at first, I swear. But as time passed, I began to wonder."

I got up from the table to pour us both coffee, then slid a cup in front of Marie. I sat down again and cut myself a big slice of pie. I'd earned it.

"Did you ever get proof?"

"No, and I never asked. I didn't want to know for sure."

I took a big bite of pie, then washed it down with some coffee. "But you're sure, anyway."

She looked down at her plate and nodded.

"It was Marge, wasn't it?"

"I think so," she said, her voice barely a whisper. "I'm so sorry to have to say that to you."

The sadness in her voice confused me. I dropped my fork on the plate and studied her. "I don't understand. I mean, I get that Harvey was no prize and your life is better with him gone, but I thought Marge was a friend of yours. She was in love with your husband and resented him for marrying you. That doesn't make you just a little angry?"

Marie looked up at me, clearly shocked. "That...I don't... Why in the world would you say that?"

"I found letters in the attic. Marge wrote them to Harvey while she was in Vietnam, but never mailed them. Tonight, I read one that referred to Harvey by name. I didn't know who she'd written them to before then."

I ran upstairs and grabbed the stack of letters from the desk in my bedroom, then hurried back downstairs and pulled out the last one I'd read and showed it to Marie as I stood beside her chair.

"See here," I said, pointing to the only passage I'd found in the letters that identified the object of her affection.

I GOT THE NEWS TODAY THAT YOU ARE TO BE MARRIED. I KNEW someone like you would not live their life out alone, but it is like a knife through my heart. Why, Harvey? The pain I feel is almost unbearable..

. . .

"She's asking him why he married you," I said. "Even if you never loved the man, it's got to be insulting on some level that your friend wanted him for herself."

Marie read the letter and her expression changed from shocked to sad again. "I guess the truth can't hurt anyone now. All this time I spent hiding and worrying..."

I slid into the chair across from her. "What truth?"

She pointed to the passage I'd identified. "That isn't a comma after 'why.' It's just a mark on the page from age or an accidental pen stroke." Marie laid the letter on the table and looked over at me.

"She wasn't asking Harvey why he'd married me," she said quietly. "She was asking me why I'd married Harvey."

"Oh." I stared at Marie. "Oh!"

Marie nodded. "I know. That sort of thing wasn't acceptable back then."

"But did you feel...did you..."

"No. I loved Marge as a friend, but I don't have those kinds of feelings for her. She knew that and accepted that we'd only ever be friends. I think if I would have married a good man—a kind man—she wouldn't have been so upset. But Harvey, well..."

"He didn't treat you well. And that made her mad."

"Yes. She tried to get me to leave him, even offered me a place to live and money, but she didn't have enough to cover Charlie's expenses. And besides, I couldn't take from her, knowing how she felt. It wouldn't have been right."

I tried to imagine how Marie felt, trapped with a mean man, dependent on him to take care of her only immediate family, but I couldn't begin to understand the depth of her despair. I was too independent—too self-sufficient—and it just couldn't compute.

No more than I could understand how Marge must have felt, loving someone all those years, knowing she was being mistreated, and unable to do anything about the love or the mistreatment. Although, I guess ultimately she did do something about the mistreatment, which is why we were all in this mess now.

"Okay, I get that Marge wouldn't have liked how you were treated, but she sat and watched it for a lot of years. What makes you think she finally killed him?"

"I'd been down with the flu for a couple of days. Marge was bringing me over a casserole so that Harvey would have his dinner on time. She wasn't the best cook, but Harvey had no taste anyway. He didn't care as long as food was on the table. But then Bones had an accident and broke his leg, and she had to rush him to the vet before she could deliver the food."

"And Harvey got mad?"

Marie nodded. "Harvey expected things to be as he wanted them all of the time. I could have been dead and he would have still expected dinner at five o'clock." She cocked her head to the side and scrunched her brow. "You know, since Harvey disappeared, I haven't eaten supper at five? Not one single day. I either eat early or much later. I never thought about it until now, but I suppose my subconscious did."

"Makes sense. So what happened?"

Marie frowned and looked down again. "He hit me, like he always did when he thought I'd screwed up. But this time, he hit me across the face. He usually only left marks on my body so I could hide them. Marge had walked across the backyards and was standing at the screen door in the kitchen when he did it. She saw it all."

"Did she kill him in your house?"

"No. She burst into the kitchen and threw the casserole in his face. Then she yelled at him to get out before she called the police. I knew she wouldn't because it would only make things worse for me, but Harvey believed her. He stomped out, threatening to kill me and her."

A rush of anger washed over me. Beaten over a casserole being late? I probably would have killed him myself if I'd been there. "So, what happened next?"

"Marge helped me clean the cut. He'd split the skin at my eyebrow. I had a black eye for a while, but since I was sick, I'd managed to avoid most people for a couple of days. Gertie and Ida Belle helped me cover it with makeup after that, enough so I could go to church on Sunday."

"Is church that important around here?"

Marie looked up at me. "It was then. You see, Harvey had already disappeared, and Ida Belle and Gertie were afraid if people knew he'd hit me that I would have been suspected of killing him. They also set up a bank account in the Bahamas and had me use Harvey's password to transfer money there so people would think he'd run off with one of his whores."

"Really?"

Ida Belle and Gertie had left out quite a bit of their part in the Harvey-disappearing story. No wonder they were so desperate to find another suspect. They knew if everyone found out Harvey had beaten Marie right before he disappeared that she'd be convicted before she was even tried. And since part of his body had turned up, it wasn't likely that Harvey had been the one moving money around, which left only Marie, with Gertie and Ida Belle in it up to their necks.

"So you've left the money sitting there all this time?" I asked.

"No. Ida Belle said we had to make it look like Harvey moved the money somewhere else, but do it in a way where it couldn't be traced. There was some complicated maneuvering from country to country, and a couple of those sketchy-looking lawyers got involved, but eventually, I used the money to buy a beach house in Tahiti."

"You're kidding."

"Not at all. Gertie, Ida Belle, and I go there every year for a month. We tell everyone else we're doing missions work in South America. We needed a reason to explain the tans."

"Of course."

Marie gave me a sheepish look. "I guess they didn't tell you all this."

"No. They left a couple of things out. Mostly, all the things that make them look bad."

Huge! They owed me huge for all the underhandedness. I started making a mental list. Gertie would owe me a pound cake every other day for my entire stay. Ida Belle was going to let me borrow her car.

"So, I take it the police bought off on Harvey running?" I asked, something about the entire thing still not making sense to me.

Marie nodded.

All of a sudden, it hit me. "Did you tell Ida Belle and Gertie about what Marge saw?"

"No. She asked me not to, and until today, I've kept her secret."

I stared, the entire mess starting to click together. "So all this time, Gertie and Ida Belle have really thought you killed Harvey?"

"Yes, but I didn't want to betray Marge. After a while, the whole thing became old news and there wasn't any reason to revisit it. Besides, Marge was protecting me. I couldn't put her at risk."

"Until now. You know the truth is going to have to come out."

"I know, but I'm afraid after all the lies, no one's going to believe me."

I blew out a breath. "Me, too."

CHAPTER EIGHTEEN

Despite being roused out of bed, Gertie and Ida Belle made it to my house within minutes of my phone call. They both wore bathrobes and slippers, and Ida Belle had a head full of rollers, but they were wide awake and clearly stunned at the turn of events.

It took a bit to explain everything to Gertie and Ida Belle, who flopped back and forth between being thrilled Marie was all right, shocked that she hadn't actually killed Harvey, and nonplussed that Marge had been in love with Marie and apparently done the deed.

"It all makes sense now," Ida Belle said, "but who would have figured?"

Gertie shook her head. "I am so sorry, Marie. All these years, we've thought you were the one that killed him."

"It's all right. I knew that's what you thought when you helped me with the offshore bank."

"But why didn't you tell us?" Gertie asked.

"She was protecting Marge," I said.

Marie nodded. "She killed Harvey to protect me. How could I let her take the fall for something I should have handled years ago myself? Especially knowing how she felt about me. It would have been a knife in her heart and her back."

"It was a big risk," Ida Belle said. "If Harvey's body had turned up before Marge died, you would have had to choose."

"I doubt it," I said. "My guess is that if Marge were still alive, she would have confessed. She'd never have let Marie go to prison. In fact, from Marie's standpoint, she'd be much better off if Marge were still here to confess. Given all the subterfuge, it's going to be hard to get people to buy off on this."

"You're probably right." Ida Belle sighed. "If only we had a way to prove all of it. Proof that a jury couldn't overlook."

Suddenly, a thought flashed through my mind. I jumped up from my chair, startling the three of them.

"Marge's estate attorney called me earlier this week. He said he had a letter that was to be delivered to me on Marge's death." I clenched Gertie's shoulder. "What if she left a confession, just in case the whole thing blew up after she died?"

Three hopeful expressions stared back at me.

"It would be just like Marge to do something like that," Gertie said. "Honor was a way of life with her."

Ida Belle nodded. "So, when can you get this letter?"

I checked my watch. "Their office opens in a couple of hours. I figure we have time to get dressed, grab some breakfast and haul butt to New Orleans to be there when it does."

Ida Belle and Gertie jumped up from their chairs.

"It's a plan," Gertie said. "We can take my car now that it's been fumigating for a day."

Ida Belle nodded. "Marie, you better stick around here. No one's caught on to your hiding place yet." She shot me a derisive look. "Including the person living in the house. You should be safe here as long as you stay out of sight. Melvin already has some misconceptions about Fortune's role here. I don't want him to catch a glimpse of you when he's sneaking around."

"I'll be back in the attic before daylight," Marie promised. "I'm just going to get a quick shower and change clothes. It will be nice to take my time in the bathroom. I've been rushing down when you left, hoping you wouldn't catch me."

Gertie frowned. "She doesn't need to hide in the attic any longer, does she?"

"It's okay," Marie said. "I'll feel safer there until y'all return. Just in case."

"She's right," I said. "I'd like to think Melvin isn't stupid enough to break into the house in broad daylight, but as I've spoken with him, I can't guarantee anything."

Gertie patted Marie's arm. "As soon as we get back with that letter, we're going to pick you up and go straight to see the sheriff. We're going to put this entire mess to bed once and for all."

I felt my back and neck tense up. There was a lot riding on a letter that we weren't even sure existed.

I hoped Gertie's prophecy was right.

———

It took every ounce of self-control I had to smile politely at Mr. Worley and appear patient as he regaled me with tales about the woman he thought was my aunt. All of a sudden, it seemed things were actually taking on that slow pace everyone claimed for small-town living. Of course, it happened at the exact time I wanted everything to move at lightning speed. Well, now and during the sermon on Sunday.

He sat across from me, in that giant leather chair that seemed to swallow up all one hundred forty-six pounds of him, holding the sacred envelope in his hand, and showing no signs of running out of things to say. I was almost ready to create an accident with my coffee so that he'd cut things off, when the receptionist poked her head in his office to tell him his next appointment had arrived. He looked at his watch in surprise, then pushed a piece of paper across the desk to me.

"I'm sorry," he said. "We've been having such a great conversation that I didn't realize how much time had passed."

Fifty-six minutes. Ten seconds. Eleven. Twelve.

"That's all right," I said and took the pen he was offering to sign the receipt document.

I pushed the paper back across to him and rose from my chair. He jumped up as well, handed me the letter, and then shook my hand for what felt like another five minutes. By the time I got out of the office, my pulse was at heart attack level. I practically ran to the curb and jumped in the back of Gertie's Cadillac.

Both ladies turned around to give me expectant stares.

"Well?" Ida Belle asked.

"I don't know yet," I said as I tore open the envelope. "He wouldn't shut up."

"Hurry up," Gertie instructed, her hands clenched together on top of the front seat.

"I'm hurrying," I muttered as I pulled the letter from the envelope and unfolded it.

Ida Belle blew out a breath as she saw the scrawl. "Thank God, she wrote it longhand. The handwriting can be verified."

"Read it already!" Gertie yelled.

I took a deep breath and started to read out loud.

SANDY-SUE,

Before I get to the point of this letter, I want to apologize for leaving this on your shoulders. If you stick around long enough to find out the particulars of the situation, you'll understand why I couldn't get any of my friends in Sinful involved.

I killed Harvey Chicoron.

When I was delivering a casserole, I saw him hit his wife, Marie. I'd always suspected that was the case, but I'd never had proof. Once I did, I saw red. I made a promise to myself that Harvey would never strike Marie again.

I knew Marie didn't have options for leaving. Without Harvey's money, she wouldn't be able to continue caring for her brother, and I knew Marie would endure any level of indignity to preserve her brother's care.

So I killed him and made it look like he'd disappeared with another woman. I knew it was the only way Marie would get the money and the quiet she deserved to live out the rest of her life.

I am sorry if my actions caused grief for anyone in Sinful after my demise, but I am not sorry for what I did.

Please show this letter to the sheriff so that suspicion no longer falls on Marie, but instead, blame is finally placed where it belongs.

Your loving aunt,

Marge

WE WERE ALL SILENT FOR SEVERAL MINUTES. TEARS POOLED in Gertie's eyes, and she sniffed, then rubbed the bottom of her nose with her finger. Ida Belle stared down at the floorboard, her grief so clear despite how hard she worked to control it.

A wave of guilt washed over me for pretending to be the family of a woman who was so clearly missed. All this time, the situation with Marie and Harvey had been like a game to me—a puzzle that needed solving. I hadn't stopped to think about the loss that had occurred to precipitate my arrival in Sinful, or how much it was still affecting these women, even though they didn't show it.

Then I felt sad. Sad for Ida Belle, Gertie, and Marie, and all the other women who'd considered Marge a neighbor and friend. Her dedication to protecting the freedom of others who couldn't protect themselves had extended far beyond her military service. I regretted that I'd never gotten to meet her when she was alive. I think I would have liked her. I already knew I respected her.

"Well," Ida Belle said, then went silent again.

"I'm sorry I didn't know her better," I said. "And I'm sorry all of you lost such a great friend."

A single tear ran out of Gertie's eye and onto her cheek. She swiped it away with her finger and then smiled at me. "She would have loved you. All that worrying she did over how you'd turn out. I think she would have been surprised and very pleased."

I felt my heart ache just a bit. Sure, I was pretending to be Marge's niece, but they didn't know that. The fact that Gertie thought Marge would have been pleased touched me. It was the first time since my mom passed that someone had given me a genuine compliment. I'd forgotten what it felt like.

"I guess we don't have to worry about Marie going to jail any longer," Gertie said.

"No," I agreed, but at the moment, it seemed small consolation.

———

THE DRIVE FROM NEW ORLEANS BACK TO SINFUL WAS A sober one, none of us having much to say. No one had thought to leave Marie a cell phone, so she wouldn't know what we'd found until we got back to Marge's house. I figured it was just as well. To read the letter over a cell phone seemed rude. It was the sort of thing that really needed to be done in person.

My thoughts whirled around on all the twists these few short days in Sinful had taken and marveled at the strength of the women I'd met and the one who had already passed.

Which got me right back to the dread I felt at showing the letter to Marie, who would probably feel guilty about it all.

It was a little after noon when we got back to Marge's house. Marie was peeking down the stairs when we walked in and hurried down to join us as soon as Ida Belle closed the blinds. The anxiety in her expression made my heart clench just a bit. How must she feel—with her freedom and her brother's financial and medical security riding on her dear friend admitting to a horrible crime? How had she lived all these years, seeing Marge every day, and both of them pretending nothing was out of sorts?

"We got it," Gertie said. "Let's have some coffee and talk."

Coffee in the afternoon sounded a bit odd with the heat of the Louisiana summer, but we'd made a single stop on our return from New Orleans to pick up a bottle of bourbon. I figured a heavy dose was going straight into Marie's cup, which certainly wasn't the worst idea I'd heard, and noticed that Gertie pulled out the decaffeinated coffee instead of the regular.

"Have you eaten today?" Gertie asked Marie after she put the coffee on to brew.

"I had a glass of orange juice," Marie said.

Gertie gave her a single nod. "I'll make some dry toast. You need to eat something. You getting sick won't help anyone."

Bones woke up and stretched, then walked over to where Marie sat, and nudged her hand. She scratched him behind the ears, and he put his chin on her leg, looking up at her with those big, sad, hound eyes.

"What's going to happen to Bones?" I asked.

Marie's eyes widened. "Well, that's up to you. You inherited him along with the rest of Marge's estate."

I flopped into a chair across the table from Marie. "Oh. I hadn't even thought about it that way." Especially as I wasn't Sandy-Sue and hadn't really inherited anything. But despite all the legalities, I was about to make an executive decision about someone else's property.

"I wouldn't dream of taking him away from here," I said. "I can't imagine he'd be happy in the city."

I looked over at Marie. "Do you want to take him?"

Marie looked down at the old hound dog and smiled. "I'd love to have him. Bones is the best man I've ever lived with."

"Got that right," Ida Belle said. "And let that be a lesson. Five more years and you're in the Sinful Ladies Society. Stick to Bones and knitting. It's safer."

I swear, the old hound must be part human, because he walked under the table and licked my hand before going back to curl up in his corner bed. I smiled, feeling better that Marie wouldn't be alone anymore. Ida Belle gave me an approving nod, and Gertie sniffed, then pretended her nose itched as she placed the dry toast in front of Marie.

"That coffee ready yet?" Ida Belle asked.

"Coming right up." Gertie said and started filling cups.

Marie picked up one of the slices of toast and took a bite, but she didn't seem enthusiastic about eating. I didn't blame her. High stress levels tended to eliminate my appetite as well, and I normally had no shortage. I saw Gertie add a generous swish of bourbon to Marie's coffee before she carried the cups to the table and took a seat.

Marie took a sip of the coffee and grimaced a little. "It's a little strong, Gertie. Pass me some sugar."

Gertie slid the sugar bowl across the table to Marie. We all sipped in silence for a couple of minutes. I figured they were waiting for Marie to eat more of the toast and get a bit of the coffee in her before hitting her with the letter.

I sipped my coffee, trying to remain patient, and was just about to give it up when Marie swallowed the last bite of toast and Gertie nodded at me. I pulled out the letter and slid it across the table to Marie. Reading it out loud to her somehow felt intrusive.

Marie hesitated, the fear clear in her expression, then finally lifted the letter and began reading. Her eyes grew red and watery as she read, and a single tear slid down her cheek as she placed the letter on the table.

"Can we wait until tomorrow to take this to the sheriff?" she asked, her voice breaking.

"Of course, dear," Gertie said and patted her hand.

Ida Belle nodded. "It's been waiting all these years. I don't think another day is going to kill anyone."

"Is this going to be enough?" Marie asked. "To, you know..."

"I think so," I said. "The police will want to talk to all of you, of course, but I can't see any reason for the prosecutor to pursue you on this. It really doesn't serve anyone's interest, including the prosecutor's. The chance of getting a conviction against you given these letters is slim. It's definitely enough to sway a jury."

"Showing all this to the sheriff is the first step, anyway," Gertie said.

"Exactly," Ida Belle chimed in. "And we'll be right there to help you with this and every step that comes after."

Marie rose from the table and gave us all a small smile. "I appreciate everything you've done. I don't know what I would have done without you. You're wonderful people, and I don't deserve such good friends. I'm going to get back out of sight, just in case Melvin is watching. I need some time to be alone with my thoughts...and talk to Marge."

I don't know why exactly, but the thought of Marie, sitting in the attic on that cot, talking to her dead friend—the woman who'd killed to save her—got me choked up. I felt the pressure building in my nose and between my eyes, and my mouth dropped a bit as I realized what was happening.

I caught the tear before it escaped my eye and stared at my moist fingers. I hadn't shed a tear since my mother's funeral twenty years ago. I wasn't sure what it said about me that I shed a tear for a woman I'd never met but hadn't shed a single tear when my father died.

"We're going to go," Gertie said, and I realized they'd risen from the table and were standing there, purses in hand, and looking down at me.

"Call if you need anything," Ida Belle said, always the one taking care of business.

But I could see the unshed tears in her eyes as well, although she was working hard to keep them in. Gertie didn't even bother trying to stop them or wipe them away, instead letting them rest on her tanned skin, like proud emotional banners.

As they left the house, I stared down at the kitchen table, wishing I could be more like Gertie.

CHAPTER NINETEEN

I TRIED TO MAKE MYSELF BUSY, BUT PUTTING UP THE COFFEE cups, cleaning the pot and wiping the kitchen table took only minutes. Then I wandered from room to room, wondering what to do with my afternoon. Marie was still tucked away in the attic, and I really didn't expect to see her for a while, if not tomorrow morning.

Packing the house was always on the list of things to do, but I still felt funny making decisions about someone else's property, and for once, I wasn't starving. Sighing, I opened the kitchen blinds that had been closed to hide Marie and stared across the back lawn to the bayou. It was deceptively peaceful, but that slow-moving, muddy water had held a secret that set off a maelstrom in this small town.

A cluster of cypress trees on the far right of the lawn perched right near the bank, the huge limbs shading the yard and part of the bayou. In the middle of the trunks hung a rope hammock. I stared at the hammock for a couple of seconds, then hurried upstairs, mind made up. I was going to grab my book, get in that hammock, and do my best to escape for a couple of hours. The next morning was going to be hard, and I needed to get centered before I went to the sheriff with the three ladies.

I took the time to change into shorts, then grabbed my book and hurried outside, not bothering with shoes. The hammock was wide and comfortable, and I settled in immediately. I hadn't managed to read a chapter before I caught myself dozing off.

My eyes had just closed when I heard the sound of a boat approaching. I didn't bother to open them. I wasn't doing anything illegal, for a change, and I figured whoever it was would continue on by, but seconds later, the engine cut out and I heard a thud on the bank in front of me.

I opened one eye and saw Ally standing in a flat-bottom boat, smiling at me.

"I was beginning to wonder if you'd heard me," she said. "Sorry I interrupted such a good nap."

I swung my legs out of the hammock and walked up to the edge of the bank. "That's okay. I was supposed to be reading, but then I got comfortable and warm and, well..."

Ally nodded. "Why do you think I'm in my boat? I just crawled out of a lawn chair with a serious case of bed head. I was supposed to be working on some pastry recipes. I figured if I didn't get upright, I'd never get back out of the chair."

"So you're cruising Sinful by boat? Is that really interesting enough to keep you awake?"

Ally laughed. "Hardly. But I thought fishing might keep me up and provide me with a nice supper and at least, a change of scenery. So, what do you say—want to hit the bayou with me?"

Fishing certainly wasn't on my list of things I liked to do, but I did like Ally, and so far, I hadn't gotten into any trouble when I was with her.

"You sure it's not going to rain?" I asked and pointed to the dark clouds in the distance.

"Probably not until tonight. That's pretty typical of Louisiana in the summer."

"Oh, why not," I decided. "Let me lock up the house. I don't have any equipment, though. Maybe Marge has some in her shed."

"Don't worry about it. I've got several poles."

I hurried inside to change into a tank top and grabbed a pair of flip-flops that I'd kicked off in the living room. They probably weren't the best choice for fishing, but I'd noticed Ally was wearing them as well, so I figured she wasn't as serious about fishing as she was about getting out of the house for a while. We were definitely on the same wavelength there. I'd much rather be outdoors whenever possible.

For a second, I wondered if I should tell Marie I was going out, but decided to leave her in peace. If she needed something, Ida Belle and Gertie were only a phone call away. I gave Bones a quick pat and hurried back outside, locking the back door behind me.

Ally gave my outfit an approving nod. "Fishing is really about getting a tan. I'm glad you thought to go sleeveless, although you've got a really good tan already, especially for being from up north. Do you use tanning beds?"

As my tanning "secret" was working in the Middle Eastern desert, I stretched my mind for an answer that made sense, but I wasn't really clear on the question. Then my mind flashed back to the Facebook page, to that vain, simpering beauty-queen who had left Sinful to become an actress.

"I have one of those lamps," I said, reciting one of her self-aggrandizing posts. "I use it in the spring so that I won't burn when I get outside in the summer."

"That's smart. A burn is no fun. Always itchy and with the humidity combined with heat around here, you're forced to stay in air-conditioning until it heals. I hate being cooped up."

I pushed the boat away from the bank and hopped in,

taking a seat on the bench across the front of the boat. "Are you sure you want to be a chef? I've never seen any baking outdoors."

She laughed. "I'm going to make sure when I build my own shop that I have huge picture windows in the baking area. Until, I plan on suffering a lot."

She started the motor and directed the boat at a cruising pace up the bayou, waving at people along the bank as she went. I closed my eyes, enjoying the feel of the wind and sun on my face. Even the smell of the muddy water seemed somehow relaxing, and I started to understand why people liked living here.

"Oh, he's a big one." Ally's voice broke me out of my half stupor, and I opened my eyes as an enormous alligator swam within inches of the boat.

"Jeez, he must be twelve feet long." I stared at the beast, whose entire body extended on top of the water as he paddled down the bayou. As he disappeared below the surface, I rethought that liking-to-live-here thing. Relaxing too much in Louisiana might get you eaten.

"I guess you don't swim much around here," I said.

"Oh, mostly they mind their own business. People ski down this bayou all the time, and kids swim off the docks."

"Do their parents have them heavily insured?"

Ally laughed. "There's an angle I never considered, but you've got me wondering as my mother let me swim off the dock, too."

She continued down the bayou past Main Street, and I looked back to see the town fading into the distance. Finally, we reached an open area and she eased the boat under a tree. She cut the engine, then reached over to pick up two fishing poles and handed me one.

"Do you know how to cast?" she asked.

"It's been a while, but I'll figure it out." I did a quick

review of the equipment and strained my mind back to the one time my father had taken me fishing. He promptly decided that, since I wasn't a boy, I wouldn't be able to do it properly.

My jaw clenched involuntarily, and I executed a perfect throw into the middle of the bayou.

Ally whistled. "Great toss. Now reel it in, and let's put some bait on it so you catch a fish."

"Oh yeah, bait," I grumbled and I reeled in the line.

Ally stuck her hand in an ice chest and handed me a shrimp and a beer. "The shrimp goes on the line," she said with a grin.

I baited the line, tossed it back out, and popped the top on the beer. "Maybe fishing isn't so bad."

"Oh, it's really an excuse to be outside and drink beer. Sometimes, I don't even bait my line. I just toss it out there and sleep."

She tossed her own line out into the bayou, then leaned back across the bench at the back of the boat. I decided that Ally was by far the smartest person I'd met in Sinful and laid back across my bench, enjoying the shade of the cypress tree and the gentle breeze that blew across the bayou.

I must have dozed off, because the next thing I remember was the sound of a roaring engine. Before I could sit up, the boat pitched on its side and I fell off the bench and into the bottom of the boat.

"Damn them!" Ally yelled from the back of the boat.

I stood up and saw a boat speeding away down the bayou away from us. "Who was that?"

"The Lowery brothers. Trust me, you don't want to know more. They're mannerless pigs. Everyone on the bayou slows down for fishermen except them."

I heard another boat engine rumble behind me and readied myself to avoid another bottom-of-the-boat experience, but as

I turned, I saw Deputy LeBlanc cut the engine on his boat and coast up beside us.

"You all right?" he asked me.

"Fine," I said.

"I'll give them a ticket," he said to Ally. "They won't pay it, but I'll have the ammunition to toss them in jail for a couple of days. I'll run them down before I head to New Orleans for an appointment."

"Good," Ally said.

He looked back at me and gave me a once-over. "I see you're keeping better company today. Hell, you're even wearing clothes. Keep up the good work."

He gave me a grin, started his engine and headed off down the bayou in pursuit of the Lowery brothers.

"He's seen you without clothes?" Ally asked, her eyes wide.

"I was wearing a trash bag, but it's sorta a long story."

Ally flopped back down on the bench. "I have a twelve-pack and the day off. *This*, I have got to hear."

———

ALLY AND I WERE HAVING SUCH A GOOD TIME, WE MANAGED to polish off six of the beers and kill the entire afternoon and some of the evening. We even caught six huge fish that Ally identified as speckled trout, and she promised to invite me over to eat. I'd finally told her about the trip to the Swamp Bar, hedging around the reason for the trip and the exact cause of my dip. She'd laughed until she cried and then laughed more.

Her sheer delight in my ultimate humiliation finally forced me to see the humor in the situation, and I laughed as well, then marveled that I'd found such a comfort level with a woman I barely knew, when I'd never found that same level of comfort with anyone back home. Hadley had known me since

I was a kid and gladly volunteered as a fill-in mom. Director Morrow, who'd been my father's partner at the time of his death, had done his best to steer me in the right direction, but I still wouldn't confide in either of them, much less volunteer up things that embarrassed me.

And all of that was so convoluted and loaded with baggage that I wasn't about to dive into analyzing it. Especially not today. On a pleasant day, with a good breeze, great company, and beer. Finally, when we were sunburned and beer-logged, Ally headed back up the bayou to Marge's house, making me promise to meet her for late breakfast the next morning.

Marie crept out of the attic when she heard me stirring downstairs, and I fixed us up grilled cheese sandwiches. She didn't say much, but I could see the weight of everything in her eyes. I didn't envy what she had to do tomorrow in the least—not even in exchange for a free pass to all of Harvey's money. A lifetime of guilt was clearly eating at her.

I had just stepped out of the shower when the text message signal on my cell phone sounded. What now? It had been so quiet all day, and I'd really hoped that would carry into tomorrow, at least until we went to see the sheriff.

I wrapped myself with a bath towel and went into the bedroom to check the message. Marie, whom I'd finally convinced to move into the spare bedroom across from me, hurried into my room.

"Who is it?" she asked.

I glanced at the display. "Gertie."

We're having trouble with the new blanket design and need your knitting expertise. Come to my house as soon as possible.

My pulse spiked and I felt the blood run from my face. Gertie and Ida Belle knew I couldn't knit. The message sent me right back to the Middle East, with all the tricks and codes Harrison and I used to let each other know we were in distress.

I knew immediately that everything about that message was wrong.

Clearly, the intent was to get me to Gertie's house.

"It's a trap," I said.

Marie's eyes widened. "What's happening?"

"We've been wrong...so very wrong." The only people who knew I was in cahoots with Ida Belle and Gertie were Walter, Deputy LeBlanc, Marie and Melvin. Only one of them had reason to want us all in the same place and be secretive about it.

And then it hit me—everything everyone had believed all these years had been off. All this running around to use Melvin as a misdirection, and he'd been the killer all along. I'd bet money on it.

"What's wrong, Fortune? Tell me what's going on." Marie's voice rose in pitch.

I dropped the phone on the bed and ran back into the bathroom to throw on my clothes; then I rushed out and pulled on my tennis shoes. Marie gasped when I pulled Marge's pistol out of the nightstand and checked the clip before tucking it into my waistband.

I hurried over to her and gripped her arms. "Listen to me. I don't know if he's back from New Orleans, but I need you to call Deputy LeBlanc and tell him that Gertie and Ida Belle are being held hostage at Gertie's house."

All the blood rushed from Marie's face. "Who's holding them hostage?"

"If I'm right—Melvin."

Marie's hands flew up to cover her mouth. "Oh, God! This is all my fault."

"You can play the blame game later. When you reach Deputy LeBlanc, tell him I've gone to help and I'm armed. Do you understand?"

"Yes," Marie said, her voice barely a whisper.

I shook her a bit. "Snap out of it, Marie. Gertie and Ida Belle need you to be strong."

Suddenly, something clicked in Marie. I could see it in her eyes.

The tears that were threatening to fall seem to evaporate. She straightened up to full height, her jaw set in a hard line, and probably for the first time in her life, Marie got mad.

"Damn right, I'll call the deputy," she said. "Now, you go shoot that son of a bitch!"

I grinned at her before running out of the house and across the street. I wanted to take a peek through Gertie's back windows before I went and rang the doorbell. If there was a way to sneak up on Melvin and get the advantage, I was taking it. No use politely stepping through a doorway into potential death unless absolutely necessary.

Silently, I lifted myself over Gertie's back fence and crept across her yard, happy that she hadn't turned on her back porch light. Only a faint glow from the moonlight reached the yard. The shadows of the hedges provided pitch-black cover all the way to the kitchen window.

I felt my pulse beating so hard that my chest felt it would explode. I concentrated on breathing, but it wasn't helping. I paused for a moment before I reached the edge of the house, trying to get a grip. What was wrong with me? This was my job. This was what I'd done for a living for the past five years, yet I felt like an agent out on my first kill.

Then it hit me like a bolt of lightning. This was personal.

I cared about the people inside that house, which made this the most important mission I'd ever been on. I couldn't afford any mistakes. Lives that mattered were on the line.

CHAPTER TWENTY

I PEERED IN THE BACK WINDOW, BUT THE KITCHEN WAS empty. The only light I could see was a dim streak coming down the narrow hallway from the living room. He was probably holding them in there and had only a lamp on. Lack of light gave him the advantage when I entered the house, and he'd have no reason to suspect that I was coming prepared for battle.

He certainly had no idea he'd just messed with the friends of a professional assassin.

Entry on the first floor was out of the question. It was too easy for him to check the downstairs rooms, and climbing through windows wasn't exactly the perfect position for gunfire—not for the one needing to fire, anyway. As I was scouting the trees in the backyard, the storm that had been threatening to break all day let loose. Lightning flashed across the sky and hit the ground with a deafening boom. The windowpanes clanked as the entire house shook. A second later, rain began pouring from the sky.

I could barely contain my excitement. The storm would hide the minor noise I'd have to make to enter the house. I hurried to a huge oak tree on the side of the house and shinnied up it to the roof. I perched on a branch and waited for the next roll of thunder, then leapt onto the roof. I scrambled to the topmost peak and leaned over the side of the house to pull on the attic window.

It was unlocked!

I lifted the window, took a deep breath, and then grabbed the window frame with both hands. In one fluid motion, I pushed myself over the edge and pulled myself straight through the window, praying that Gertie didn't have anything sharp or breakable stored beneath it. I landed shoulders first on a stack of cardboard boxes. They split immediately under my weight, but squished silently to the ground, the clothes they contained masking the sound of my fall.

So far, everything had been perfect. I vacillated between hoping it was all meant to be and worrying that my lucky streak was going to run out at the worst time possible. The attic floor presented the first set of obstacles I needed to overcome. The houses were well-constructed but old and creaky.

I pulled off my tennis shoes to reduce the sound of footsteps, but nothing short of the ability to hover was going to reduce my weight on the floor. I waited for the next set of thunder, then hurried across the floor to the attic stairs. I pushed the attic door open and breathed a sigh of relief when the well-oiled hinges didn't make a sound. The low rumble of thunder was still echoing outside, so I eased down the steps, pausing every time a step made even the slightest creak.

I stopped at the landing for the second floor and put my ear to the door, listening for any activity. I didn't hear a thing. Hoping they were on the first floor, I eased the door open and peeked into the hallway. It was clear.

I slipped into the hallway and glided toward the stairwell, my sock-covered feet silently moving across the wooden floor.

At the stairwell, I lay down and leaned over the edge to peer into the living room.

It wasn't good. Ida Belle sat on the couch against the front wall, both her hands and legs bound with rope. She was stiff as a board, and for the first time since I'd met her, she looked disconcerted. Gertie was in a chair in the middle of the room, her hands and legs tied. A dark bruise was already forming across her cheek, and I felt my blood boil at the sight.

Melvin stood in front of her, a shotgun leveled at her head.

"Where is she?" he yelled at Gertie. "You sent that message over ten minutes ago, and she's right around the corner."

"Maybe she was in the shower or asleep, or not even home," Gertie said. "If you'd let me call instead of text, I could have found out."

"No way was I giving you the opportunity to tip her off. If I see any sign of the cops, I'm shooting first and getting the hell out of here."

"You're not going to get away with this," Ida Belle said.

Melvin sneered. "You stupid bitch. I've gotten away with killing Harvey for five years now. If you broads hadn't hid the body, Marie would be rotting in prison, and I'd be somewhere in the Bahamas with all my cousin's money."

"You couldn't have killed Harvey," Ida Belle said. "You were in prison. Stop taking credit for things you didn't do."

"Another word from you, and I'll shoot you on principle. I came up with the plan. I found a partner that could carry it out without a hitch. Pulling a trigger is the easy part."

"So, how do you plan on explaining killing all of us?" Gertie asked. "Don't you think the police will wonder?"

"Oh, that's the best part," he said with a smile. "After Marie disappeared, I took this shotgun from her house. It has Harvey's name engraved on the side. Everyone will think Marie killed you to keep you from telling she killed Harvey.

Her disappearing makes everything perfect. No alibi she comes up with will be good enough for the police now."

I picked my head back up and took in a deep breath. I blew it slowly out, trying to calm myself and form a plan. Melvin's idea was simple and diabolically accurate. Marie wouldn't have a bit of defense, especially if the three of us, the only people who could provide her an alibi, were dead. Even Marge's letter wouldn't hold weight against three bodies and a murder weapon.

The only glimmer of light in the entire mess was the thought that Marge hadn't killed anyone after all. She must have found Harvey's body after Melvin's partner did the deed, and thinking Marie had done it, hid the body in the swamp. She left the confession letter, hoping to buy Marie a pass when she died.

I shook my head at the complexity of the situation all these women had created because they all thought another of them had killed Harvey and were all trying to cover it up. With friends like that, you could conquer small countries.

At the moment, I needed to conquer only a small living room...without anyone dying. Unless it was Melvin. My mind flashed back to that bruise on Gertie's cheek. I would enjoy killing Melvin but it would definitely make my situation more difficult. I shook my head. Who was I kidding? Killing Melvin would blow my cover altogether, but I could deal with that later.

First up, I had to get into the living room without Melvin seeing me.

I rolled over onto my back and stared up at the ceiling, trying to think of something that would distract Melvin long enough for me to get into the living room. I glanced at the table above me and saw a large crystal vase. Instantly, an idea formed.

I rose silently from the landing and lifted the vase from the table. It was thick and heavy, and, I hoped to God, not a family heirloom. The other side of the spiral staircase opened up to the formal dining room, located off the far side of the living room from Ida Belle and Gertie. I peeked into every corner of the downstairs rooms that I could see, but there was no sign of Melvin's partner in crime, Cheryl. Maybe she'd been wise and sat this one out.

I pulled off my socks for better running grip, then heaved the vase over the stairwell and onto the middle of the dining table. Before the vase even connected with anything, I was already back on the floor, leaning over the edge of the stairs. The vase crashed onto the table, and the sound echoed through the house.

The instant Melvin ran to the dining room to investigate, I flipped over the stairs and landed in the living room. Gertie and Ida Belle's eyes widened, but they didn't even flinch, much less utter a sound. Before Melvin could even turn around, I had my pistol trained on him.

"Don't even think about moving," I said as he spun around to stare at me. "I want you to place that shotgun on the ground, nice and easy."

Melvin hesitated for a couple of seconds, and I know he was weighing his options. He must have decided it wasn't worth the risk, because he placed the shotgun on the floor and stood back up with his hands raised.

"You're making a big mistake," he said.

"Really? It doesn't look that way from where I'm standing."

I heard the movement in the hallway to the kitchen too late to respond as Cheryl stepped into the living room, her nine millimeter aimed directly at Gertie's head.

"Guess I got here just in time," Cheryl said.

She looked over at me. "You could shoot me, but I'll probably get one off before you pull the trigger. And before you weigh your choices, I want to tell you that I'm a prison guard.

I spend hours at the range each week. I'm not another white-trash fool from this hick town."

"Yes, you are," Ida Belle grumbled.

"Shut up, you old hag!" Cheryl screamed. "You two think you're so important, lording over everyone in this town. I bet people will be glad to be rid of you, even if they wouldn't say it to your face."

She motioned to me with her other hand. "Put that pistol on the floor and kick it over to me. No funny stuff or Gertie gets it."

I hesitated, trying to buy even a second of time to come up with an idea. Relinquishing my weapon was useless as they were going to kill us anyway. The only way we were coming out of this alive was if I could figure out a way to disarm Cheryl before Melvin could grab the shotgun. I glanced at the accent table next to Cheryl and saw Gertie's knitting basket sitting there.

And an idea formed.

"Hurry up!" Cheryl yelled.

I glanced at Gertie and Ida Belle. They both gave me a small nod. They knew the score as well as I did, and I decided the nod was their way of telling me to take my best shot, even if it was a long one.

I leaned over and placed the pistol on the floor.

"Kick it to me," Cheryl said.

I took a breath and edged my foot next to the pistol. When I pushed it across the floor, Cheryl looked down, as I'd figured she would, and I launched. Before she could even get fixed on me, I dove for her middle, grabbing a knitting needle from the basket next to her as I tackled her to the ground. She swung her nine around toward my head as we fell to the floor, but before she could squeeze the trigger, I stabbed the knitting needle right through her jugular.

She gasped as blood spurted from her throat, but her grip

was still tight on the pistol that I struggled to pull from her grasp.

I looked up in time to see Melvin break out of his shocked stance and dive for the shotgun. Before he reached it, Gertie jumped up from her chair and kicked him right across the face. He staggered back a step, then launched forward and slugged her in the jaw. She went down and he grabbed the shotgun.

As Melvin swung the shotgun up to shoot me, Cheryl finally released her grip on the gun. I yanked the pistol from her hand and fired a single shot through Melvin's forehead. The shotgun fired as he fell to the floor, but thankfully, the shot went over my head and only took out the chandelier in the dining room. Gertie ran to the kitchen for a knife and cut the ropes loose from Ida Belle's hands and feet as I checked Cheryl's pulse. Then Ida Belle cut the ropes from Gertie's still-bound hands.

Checking for a pulse was a technicality, really. The vacant stare and the mass of blood spread across Gertie's floor were a clear indication that Cheryl was long gone from this world.

"Is she dead?" Ida Belle asked, rubbing her wrists.

"Yeah." I rose from the floor.

"How did you get in?" Gertie asked.

"I climbed up a tree and lowered myself in through an attic window. That was some kick. How did you get the ropes undone?"

"I had my legs crossed when Melvin tied me up. He's stupid. I knew I could slide them off, I was just waiting for the right moment, but my options were limited."

"And the kick?"

"Oh, that was nothing," Gertie said. "I see it all the time on those old Bruce Lee movies. I figured we had nothing to lose, right?"

She wouldn't look me in the eye, and I knew something

was up, but before I could ask, I heard a low rumble coming up the block.

I froze. "Deputy LeBlanc! I told Marie to call and tell him you were being held hostage."

I glanced at the two bodies and a wave of dizziness passed over me.

Shit!

This was so not good. There was no way I was getting out of this without being fingerprinted, logged into the system, and investigated. It would totally blow my cover, not to mention probably cost me my job.

"Run!" Ida Belle yelled.

"What?"

Ida Belle grabbed the pistol from me and fired it into the couch. I stared at her as if she'd lost her mind.

"You don't need to be in the middle of this," Ida Belle said.

Gertie nodded and pulled me toward the back door. "Shove that bloody jacket in my compost pile. Get a good soaking, then try to break in the back door when you hear us let Carter in the front door."

"But how will you explain—"

"We'll figure it out," Ida Belle said. "Go. Now!"

I scrambled through the kitchen, grabbing a butter knife as I passed the counter, then ran out the back door into the blinding storm, shrugging off my jacket as I went. I shoved the jacket into the compost pile in the corner of the yard, then circled around to the back door again. I stuck the butter knife in the doorjamb and pretended to be jimmying the back door.

Suddenly, the door flew open and Gertie looked out at me.

"Where's Melvin?" I whispered, getting into my role of knowing nothing, just in case Deputy LeBlanc was listening.

"He's dead. Get inside before you drown."

I hurried inside and followed Gertie to the living room, where Deputy LeBlanc was frowning down at the two bodies and shaking his head. The table that held the knitting basket and the chair that Gertie had been tied to were both several feet closer to Cheryl's body. A second chair had been pulled from the dining room and lay on the floor next to the first one, but none of the ropes that had bound the women were in sight.

"Do you know how lucky you two are?"

Ida Belle nodded. "We knew once Sandy-Sue arrived, they'd kill us all. But when they got to fighting over the inheritance, I knew it was our only chance to try something. When Gertie gave me the nod, I waited for the right moment."

Gertie jumped in. "As soon as Melvin put down that shotgun and came across the room to argue with Cheryl, I knew that was my chance. I grabbed the needle and shoved it in her neck."

"When Gertie stabbed her," Ida Belle continued, "I jumped up and grabbed her pistol when she dropped it."

"Melvin got a hold of his shotgun," Gertie said, her expression animated, "but Ida Belle clipped him before he got a lock on us. It was just like the county fair, only she wasn't shooting clay pigeons."

Ida Belle nodded. "Just like it. Anyway, he pulled the trigger after I shot him. Must have been some involuntary thing, but lucky for us it happened as he was falling, so the chandelier caught the worst end of it."

Gertie waved a hand. "I've always hated that chandelier."

I stared at the two of them, completely dumbfounded at how eloquently and efficiently they'd fabricated a completely plausible story and then delivered it as if it had really happened that way. This was better acting than any movie I'd ever seen.

I stepped in between them and reached out to squeeze both their shoulders. "I am so glad the two of you are all right. When I got that text, I knew something was wrong. I figured if I knocked on the front door and strolled in, we'd all be in trouble. I was trying to open the back door with a butter knife, but it wasn't cooperating."

I stared down at the bodies and shook my head. "The whole thing is unbelievable."

Deputy LeBlanc sighed. "Welcome to Louisiana."

"Ha. Yeah, I didn't quite count on this much excitement. I was under the apparently mistaken impression that small towns were quiet."

"It's a common mistake," Deputy LeBlanc said. "So, I guess since I received the rescue call from Marie, that she's returned from yonder hiding place?"

"Jesus, we forgot to call Marie!" Gertie ran off toward the kitchen, no doubt to call Marie and tell her the five-year nightmare was over for good.

"Actually," I said, "Marie never left. She was sorta living in my attic."

He stared. "And I'm supposed to believe you didn't know?"

"I didn't know. I swear. Not until today."

"So, was she playing dead? Because these houses do make noise when people move around upstairs."

I threw up my hands. "Yes, there was noise, but I thought it was the raccoon. And I wasn't about to go up there again and check after the hassle you gave me the first time."

His lips quivered just a bit, and I knew he was trying not to smile. "I didn't hassle you about checking the noise. I hassled you about trying to *shoot* the noise."

"Whatever. It translated to the same thing to me."

"Well, given that last time you shot the roof, I guess Marie was lucky you left well enough alone. So, what's this text that got you all suspicious?"

I pulled my cell phone from my pocket and showed him the text. "I knew something was wrong because Gertie and Ida Belle know I can't knit. And since we'd seen Melvin with

Marie's cousin at the Swamp Bar, I was afraid he'd gotten to them, thinking we were onto him."

"Uh-huh. You three and your investigation are something we'll discuss at length as soon as I work up the energy. I'm just wondering, though, what if it really was a knitting emergency, and you'd just panicked?"

I shrugged. "Then I would have wasted your time and almost drowned myself for no good reason, but it was a risk I was willing to take."

The smile broke through. "Well, as that's one of the only things you've done this week that wasn't illegal, I suppose this is progress."

I just smiled back and nodded. If he only knew.

A car door slammed out front, and Deputy LeBlanc went to the door to let in the parade of paramedics. I joined Ida Belle and Gertie to peek out the front window. All over the block, people started coming out of their homes and gathering in front lawns.

"Everybody's coming outside now that the cops are here," Gertie said. "Wasn't no one coming outside when they heard gunfire, though."

"Cowards," Ida Belle yelled out the front door.

I grinned. It was hard not to like the old girls.

CHAPTER TWENTY-ONE

IT WAS LONG AFTER MIDNIGHT BEFORE DEPUTY LEBLANC, the coroner, and an assortment of other people finished up at Gertie's house. I knew they'd still have a load of questions to answer and papers to sign in the coming days, but I was confident that we were safe. Deputy LeBlanc hadn't shown any hesitation in buying their story. In fact, I think he was relieved that Marie hadn't killed Harvey as he had been dreading arresting her. Melvin wasn't liked by anyone, so the entire town would probably breathe a sigh of relief and have something to talk about for the next forty years.

Marie had rushed over after Gertie called, crying like a baby and hugging everyone within an inch of their lives, including Deputy LeBlanc, who seemed a bit embarrassed by all the fuss.

When she got to me, she'd whispered in my ear, "I wish Marge could have seen you now. She would have loved you."

After the last car pulled out of the driveway and Deputy LeBlanc crossed the road to his house, I looked around at the mess in Gertie's living room and shook my head.

"Grab a change of clothes," I told Gertie. "You're staying

with me tonight."

Gertie started to protest, but Ida Belle stopped her. "She's right. We'll all help you deal with this in the daylight. But right now, we need to get out of this house."

"I know you two have your own places," I said to Ida Belle and Marie, "but I have plenty of room if you want to come as well."

Gertie clapped her hands. "Slumber party. I haven't had one of those since I was a little girl."

Ida Belle frowned. "Grown women do not have slumber parties. This will be a gathering of the troops."

I nodded. "I say the first thing we do is gather in my kitchen for coffee and whatever Gertie has baked."

Gertie lifted a chocolate cake off the kitchen counter. "What are we waiting for?"

The mood was festive as I served the coffee and Gertie cut off slices of her fabulous chocolate cake for everyone. When we were all seated at the table, Marie cleared her throat.

"I just want to tell you all," Marie said, "how much I appreciate everything you've done for me, now and in the past. And I want to apologize to Gertie and Ida Belle for not telling you that I suspected Marge had killed Harvey all those years ago. I guess Marge thought I'd done it, and we've all been covering for someone else this whole time."

"You were protecting Marge," Ida Belle said, "and we respect that. Besides, even if we'd known, it wouldn't have changed what we did. We needed to divert suspicion from you, regardless, because you were going to be the first suspect when Harvey came up missing. It didn't matter who killed him."

Relief passed over Marie's face. "I guess you're right. I just never thought about it in that light."

I looked at Marie. "So, do you have any idea when or where Harvey was killed?"

Marie nodded. "I think he was killed right in my kitchen.

I'd been sick, remember? After Harvey hit me and Marge tended to the cut, she gave me a sleeping pill and put me to bed. I was out in seconds and slept hard. I remember when I went downstairs to the kitchen later on that evening, there was the faint smell of bleach. I just brushed it off as Marge cleaning up. I mean, until later, when I started to wonder."

Ida Belle shook her head. "She was cleaning up all right—after Melvin and Cheryl—and thinking you'd done it. I bet she had the shock of her life, coming back to the house and finding Harvey dead on the kitchen floor."

"I can't even imagine," Marie said. She reached into her pocket and pulled out the letter I'd gotten from the attorney.

"As much as I'd like to keep this," Marie said, "to remind me that someone I respected and cared about loved me this much, we need to destroy this letter and all the others."

I nodded. "They would only muddy the waters if they came to light."

I got up from the table and pulled a cast-iron pot from the cabinets, then picked up the stack of unmailed letters and dropped them inside. I took the letter from Marie, then tossed it in with the others and set them on fire. Marie stood to watch them burn and then dumped the ashes in the sink and washed away any sign that the letters had ever existed.

"I think I've had about all I can take for one day," Marie said, "so if you ladies don't mind, I'm going to bed."

Ida Belle and Gertie showed no signs of retiring, so I refilled all our coffee mugs and sat down again. The adrenaline still running through me was a more potent stimulant than the coffee ever could be, and I knew it would be hours before I'd be able to relax enough to sleep.

Ida Belle looked over at Gertie with that secret look they share when they seem to talk telepathically. Gertie nodded, so I guess whatever was going on between the two of them, they were finally going to share.

"We need to talk," Ida Belle said to me.

"Okay. About what?"

"About who you really are."

I froze, not even breathing. "I don't understand," I managed to say, happy my voice sounded normal.

Gertie reached over and placed her hand on mine. "We're not interested in 'outing' you, dear. We want to protect you."

Ida Belle nodded. "But we can't do that properly if we don't know what we're protecting you from."

"We thought at first," Gertie said, "that you might be running from an abusive husband or something of the like, but once we got to know you, we knew that couldn't be the case. An abusive man wouldn't last five minutes around you."

I shook my head. "What makes you think I'm not exactly who I say I am?"

Gertie laughed. "You have fake hair, never wear makeup, and don't seem the least bit interested in clothes."

Ida Belle nodded. "You sit and stand with your back to the wall and facing openings in all buildings. You jumped an eight-foot fence like it was a speed bump, and despite your fight with Tiny, you weren't the least bit winded."

"You run like a sprinter," Gertie continued, "and have balance like a cat with the moves of an advanced martial artist. I know the construction of my attic, and no way did you 'lower' yourself into that window."

"When you meet people for the first time," Ida Belle continued, "you immediately size them up, looking for weaknesses. You single-handedly took out two armed assailants, one with a knitting needle, and the second with a pistol shot right through the center of the forehead, all done without preparation and while scrambling. Normal people think; they don't react like that."

Gertie nodded. "Throughout this entire mess of murder, kidnappings, and gunfire, you have remained nonplussed."

"The bottom line," Ida Belle said, "is that we recognize one of ours when we see them. You may not be in the military, but you've had military training, and plenty of it."

I stared at them, shocked for probably the first time in my life. I expected suspicion from Deputy LeBlanc, but I doubt even he would have come up with the detailed analysis the two innocent-looking old ladies sitting at my kitchen table had.

One of ours.

My mind locked on that statement, and I looked back and forth between the two of them. "Are you saying you two were in the military?"

"Of course," Ida Belle said. "The five founding members of the Sinful Ladies Society were all military. Me, Gertie and Marge were the last until recently, when Marge passed. Now, it's just me and Gertie."

And suddenly it dawned on me. "You all served in Vietnam together."

Gertie nodded. "It was a horrible war, but all of us felt our place was there serving our country, not back in Sinful serving some clueless man his supper."

"So, what did you do? I mean, what were your jobs?"

"Can't you guess?" Ida Bell asked.

They grinned at each other and looked at me in anticipation.

"I'm afraid to."

Ida Belle laughed. "Well, on paper, Gertie was a secretary. I was a nurse's aide. Marge was an inventory clerk."

"But that wasn't what you really did..."

Ida Belle shook her head. "You have to understand, it was a different time then—women, in particular, were viewed as a weaker sex and incapable of the same things as men. Our commander took advantage of that, used it to make strategic moves."

Suddenly, clips from the past five days flashed through my

mind like a YouTube video: Ida Belle shooting the alligator, Gertie and her Bruce Lee kick to Melvin's head, Marge's weapon collection.

I felt my jaw drop open and I stared.

Finally, I managed to speak. "You were counterintelligence."

"We prefer 'spies,'" Ida Belle said.

Gertie nodded. "It sounds cooler."

I leaned back in my chair and blew out a breath. "Spies. I can't believe it."

I narrowed my eyes at Gertie. "You're not woolly-headed or clumsy, are you?"

Gertie laughed. "Of course not."

"Well...," Ida Belle interjected.

"Am not!"

"You're not as sharp as you used to be, and that's all I'm saying."

Gertie glared at Ida Belle, then looked back at me. As soon as she turned, Ida Belle looked at me and shook her head.

"The thing I learned," Gertie said, "is that if people believe I'm clueless, they'll say and do all manner of things in front of me, thinking it doesn't matter."

I looked at Ida Belle. "And I guess that story about your dad teaching you to shoot was a lie?"

Ida Belle shook her head. "Daddy was real and as big a son of a bitch as we described him to be. I was already a good shot when I enlisted, but the military honed the skill to a level of precision that only another marksman would understand." She gave me a shrewd look.

"You're right," I said, trying to decide how much information to give and how much to hold back. Not because I didn't trust them, but because I didn't want to put them in danger.

"You know," Gertie said gently, "we're not going to appear

any more threatening to the enemy if we know the truth than if we don't."

She was right and I knew it, but I'd spent my entire life trusting no one. Making a leap of faith was a huge step for me.

"I'm not military, but they did train me. I work for the CIA."

Gertie clapped her hands. "A spook! Right here in Sinful. Imagine that."

I smiled. "No more unlikely than a ladies society run by Vietnam counterintelligence."

"She has a point," Ida Belle said, then looked at me, her expression serious. "I'm not going to ask your job description, because I think we already have a good idea, and speaking about it isn't necessary. And I'm going to assume that you didn't kill Sandy-Sue to take her place here, but I would like to know that she's safe and what exactly you're hiding from."

"Sandy-Sue is definitely safe. She's on extended vacation paid for by her uncle, who is also my boss. She knows nothing about any of this."

"Good," Ida Belle said, completely satisfied with my explanation.

"I'm hiding here because some very bad guys have a price on my head, and my boss is afraid a leak at the CIA blew my cover. I wasn't supposed to return from my last mission."

Gertie frowned. "So you're completely off-grid?"

"Yes. My boss and one other agent are the only people who know where I am. Well, and now you guys."

Gertie whistled. "And if Deputy LeBlanc looks too closely into Sandy-Sue's background, he may find out she's not here, and it would leave you exposed. We figured it was something along those lines. That's why we sent you outside after you rescued us and made up that story."

I nodded. "If I get called to testify, I'm perjuring myself just by stating Sandy-Sue's name."

"And these bad guys that are after you—what are we on the lookout for?" Ida Belle asked.

"Arms dealers. Trust me, they'd stick out in Sinful like a spotlight."

"Middle Eastern?" Gertie asked. "You're very tan...."

I nodded.

"That makes it easier," Ida Belle said.

"From now on," Gertie said, "we'll do our best to keep you out of things that put you on Deputy LeBlanc's radar."

I felt a tiny sliver of fear run through me. "Is there that much questionable activity going on in Sinful?"

"No, of course not," Ida Belle said, then winked at Gertie.

I put my hands over my ears and rose from the table. "I don't want to know," I said as I headed upstairs for a well-deserved hot shower. I could still hear them laughing when I stepped onto the second-floor landing.

I paused for a moment, smiling as their laughter traveled up the stairwell. They were good people, strong women, and loyal friends. They'd restored some of my faith in mankind, and it had cost me only a chunk of fake hair and a little embarrassment.

Not a bad accomplishment for less than a week.

For more adventure with Fortune and the girls, check out Lethal Bayou Beauty.

For information on new releases, please sign up for my newsletter at my website janadeleon.com.

ABOUT THE AUTHOR

New York Times, USA Today, and Wall Street Journal bestselling author Jana DeLeon was raised in southwest Louisiana among the bayous and gators. Her hometown is Carlyss, but you probably won't find it on a map.

Jana has never stumbled across a mystery or a ghost like her heroines, but she's still hopeful.

www.janadeleon.com